DREAD WATCH

Jared Agard

CHICKEN SCRATCH BOOKS
WWW.CHICKENSCRATCHBOOKS.COM

D0311469

Chicken Scratch Books
PO Box 104
Wisdom, MT 59761

www.chickenscratchbooks.com

Publisher's Note: This is a work of fiction. Names, characters, places, and incidents are a product of the author's imagination. Locales and public names are sometimes used for atmospheric purposes. Any resemblance to actual people, living or dead, or to businesses, companies, events, institutions, or locales is completely coincidental.

Ordering Information: Special discounts are available on quantity purchases by corporations, associations, and others. For details, contact the publisher at the address above.

First Chicken Scratch Books Printing, 2021

ISBN 978-1-953743-06-0 (paperback)
ISBN 978-1-953743-07-7 (ebook)

Printed in the United States of America

To my mom, Joy Martinelli. You were the first person who ever told me I should be an author. I love you!

"The fiend that preys and feasts on fear,
who fills your heart with dread and death,
grows stronger as your heart fades dim,
steals courage and your final breath."

-Quoted by Ed Creedy on www.deadandliving.com
Original author unknown

July 17th, 1856

Philadelphia, Pennsylvania

4 AM

Grandma Barnett's chair creaked as she rocked back and forth in front of the crackling fire. She was always up early. Always cold.

Pa crouched in front of the brick stove, giving the blaze a final poke. "Ready to go?"

"Yessir." Will wore his Sunday best: brown slacks, suspenders, and a crisp white shirt. He tugged at his bow tie with a shaky hand.

"Well. That girl's really done a number on ya, hasn't she, son?" The grizzled old farmer flashed a rare half-smile at the nervous seventeen-year-old.

Will didn't know why his face even bothered to

flush anymore. Everyone in town knew. The train ride and picnic would be a chance to spend a whole day with Anna. Seeing her at church once a week wasn't nearly enough.

Grandma cleared her throat. "He shouldn't go."

"Not this again," Will muttered. Pa went back to stoking the fire.

"Steam engine. Bah!" Grandma Barnett's wrinkled knuckles whitened from her tight grip on the armrests. "I'd not go near one of those evil machines. Fueled by the fires of hell, they are." The reflection of orange flames from the stove danced in her greyed-out eyes. "If the demons that turn the wheels don't end you, then the idleness that creeps into your bones will."

******

After a bumpy buggy ride into town, Will stepped out onto the wooden platform at Cohocksink Depot. The station was packed, the storm of young voices nearly deafening. Most of the kids were younger than Will, bright-eyed with excitement despite the hour. The sun peeked over the horizon, its deep orange light accenting hundreds of faces.

But not Anna's.

Thirteen slow, complaint filled minutes went by.

"Why's it so late?"

"It's not coming."

"This is the worst."

"Where's the train?"

Forget the train. Where's Anna?

The tracks rumbled. A black speck shone on the horizon. The children broke out in a cheer. The Shakamaxon chugged toward them, coughing clouds of smoke into the pale sky. The brakes squealed as the train slid up to the platform, the air thick with the smell of fire and iron.

The glossy locomotive *could've* been some kind of metal demon with its single eye and fang-like grin. Grandma Barnett would've probably had a heart attack at the sight of it.

Hiiiissssss. White geysers of steam crept up around the sides of the train engine like ghosts rising from their graves. A bead of sweat formed on Will's forehead.

That sound.

Hiiiiissssss. Will wiped his brow on his shirtsleeve. Just blow-off from the engine. Nothing to be afraid of.

The mist coiled as it rose, its sleek form slithering up the side of the train. Slick scales slid over the engineer's window. Will froze. A smoky forked tongue flicked out of the mouth of the serpent.

Will clenched his eyes shut. He tried to breathe. In a flash he was five years old again, his hand outstretched toward the gunnysack of goat feed, a rattling in his ears. He braced himself, but the strike of fangs never came. No pulse of venom into his bloodstream.

He opened his eyes. The very normal plume of steam spread out like a bed sheet on a clothesline and evaporated into the sky.

Scowling, Will wiped his brow again.

The engineer pulled the whistle, its shrill voice piercing the air. The children went silent.

"All aboard!"

A hand slipped into Will's. It was soft and warm but too small to be Anna's. He looked to his left and was met by two shimmering blue eyes and a wide smile.

"Hi, Will."

"Oh, uh, hello there, Ms. Kensington."

Seven-year-old Grace Kensington's smile widened. She bobbed up and down, her blond ringlets coiling and uncoiling like springs.

"Are you excited to go on the train?"

Will didn't get a chance to answer. A massive hand landed on his shoulder.

"Is my Gracie safe with you, William?" Mr. Kensington was a bricklayer and friend of Will's father. Every inch of him was heavy and jagged. Will knew the man only had one soft spot: His little girl.

"Yes, Mr. Kensington."

"Good. I didn't want her ridin' in this contraption alone. I told her to stick close to you. Your pa raised a good young man, and I know you'll bring my Gracie back to me safe and sound." He leaned down and kissed Grace's head making sure to keep his dusty overalls away from her perfectly pressed summer dress. "I'll see you soon, darlin'. Stay with Will. Don't wander off."

"Bye Daddy." Grace waved. The bear of a man smiled.

"Safe and sound. Right, Will?"

"You have my word, sir."

Mr. Kensington nodded. "Good luck with Anna today."

Will's face burned. Mr. Kensington chuckled as he walked off.

The crowd shuffled onto the train, filling each car and then stuffing in more. Grace pulled Will to the very front. They pushed their way into the car closest to the engine, so close they could even see the conductor.

Tick, tick, tick, tick. . . .

Strange. As the conductor checked his gold pocket watch, Will was sure he could hear its ticking above all of the clamor around him. Impossible.

Tick, tick, tick, tick. . . .

"Isn't this exciting?" Grace stood on her tiptoes to see out of the window, her hands on the sill.

Forget the watch. Will scanned the crowd. Anna wasn't coming. *Of course not. A train ride? That's for little kids.* She probably thought the whole thing was childish.

"Look at the chimney! Did you know trains have chimneys?"

Will followed Grace's gaze down the slope of the smokestack. It connected to the boiler, an iron bulge burning so hot the edges were blurred by heat waves.

The conductor bent down to check a gauge.

A snake's tail slipped from his jacket's pocket. Will stepped backward. The tail arched skyward and shivered. A dry rattle filled Will's ears. The blood left his face.

But it wasn't a snake's tail. It was just a chain, the chain of the gold watch hanging from the conductor's pocket.

Will rubbed his eyes.

"Did you hear that?" Grace's lower lip quivered.

"What?" Had she heard the rattling, too?

"Buzzing. Like... wasps. I... I... don't like wasps."

"There're no wasps, Gracie. All I saw was–" Will stopped himself. The summer sun was beating down on them, plus the heat from the boiler. Maybe all those extra degrees were causing hallucinations.

"There's nothing to be scared of, Gracie. This is going to be fun." Will squeezed her hand. She looked at the conductor, cautiously, like he might sting her.

"Okay." Grace turned back toward the window.

"We're ready to go," shouted the conductor. He pulled on a string and a whistle screeched.

"Got room for one more?"

Bodies scrunched in even tighter around Will. The gate on their cart slammed shut as the last person pushed into the packed train.

Anna.

Will stared at her, his mouth wide open. She was only about four feet away from him, standing as close to the wall as she could. Her dress was bright yellow, like sunshine. She smiled at Reverend Sheridan and wished him a good morning.

"Oh good. Anna's here. Now you can tell her you love her." Grace laughed.

The train lurched forward. Will had heard a steam train could go ten times faster than a horse, but that was nothing. His heart was beating faster than one thousand horses.

*****

It took some time for Will to build up his nerve. About an hour and fourteen minutes to be exact.

"We'll be at the station soon. Now or never!" Grace prodded. Will leaned closer to Anna. She stared out at the hillside, the lace trim on her sleeves dancing in the wind.

"Anna?"

She turned to him.

"Oh. Hello, Will." Her cheeks flushed, eyes sparkling.

Will looked at the floor.

"I was wondering. . . I was. . . ."

Train whistles blared, echoing around the hillside. Not just one.

Two whistles.

Two trains.

Will's attention snapped away from Anna and to the black, gleaming form that appeared from around the corner, weaving toward them like a snake.

Metal screeched against metal. Orange sparks leaped from the track. The whistles cried out.

A choir of screams.

The trains slammed into each other. Will toppled forward, his forehead smashing against the front of the cart. He grabbed onto the window ledge as the momentum ripped backward. Anna and Grace rolled into the mass of screaming children.

Will clenched his eyes shut. This couldn't be happening.

This was a nightmare.

His skull shook from the forceful blast of noise, two massive beasts roaring in agony. He forced his eyes open.

Blood and pain clouded his vision. The conductor disappeared in a wad of crumpled metal. The boilers of the two trains collided, unleashing the fires of hell. The world around Will disintegrated.

The explosion was so loud it could be heard from miles away.

But for Will, all was dark and silent.

And then, one sound . . . .

Tick, tick, tick, tick . . . .

CHAPTER 1

Tick, tick, tick, tick. . . .

I checked the time on my cell phone. Almost nine. What was taking them so long?

Moonlight dripped through the clouds and highlighted the mossy walls of the abandoned railroad museum.

Tick, tick, tick, tick. . . .What was making that annoying sound? I guessed it was coming from an old-fashioned clock. A big one. Like a clock tower. I checked around the exterior for the source of the sound but didn't see anything. It was pretty dark, so it easily could've been hidden in the shadows.

A metal plaque was bolted into the decaying wood, barely readable in the dark.

In honor of Mary Ambler.

Ambler. Just like the name of the city, or borough, I

guess. Ambler, Pennsylvania.

After my dad's accident, we'd moved here from Los Angeles. Hollywood. Sunshine. A nice condo and my dad's sports car.

Then, just like that, Ambler, Pennsylvania, and what my history teacher called "railroad heritage."

And here was their museum, their badge of pride, closed and likely condemned.

But I wasn't at the museum for a history lesson. I was here for revenge.

I moved around the corner of the building and crouched behind some frost-glazed bushes in the dark, waiting as patiently as I could.

Tick, tick, tick, tick. . . .

There was still no clock in sight. Where was that sound coming from? Maybe the other side of the building?

The foil body of my balloon crinkled as it was battered by a gust of wind. I tugged it back into hiding by its obnoxious purple ribbon. The words *Happy Birthday* were printed in blocky, multicolored letters across the front, surrounded by bursts of confetti. I'd told my mom I was going to a birthday party to get her to drop me off nearby the old museum. I had to lie. If I'd told her what I was really up to, she'd have never brought me.

My wait was plagued by freezing wisps of wind and

constant ticking. My nose was running and I couldn't keep my teeth from chattering.

And then, finally, footsteps on wet pavement.

My patience had paid off.

Blake Krebbs led the way, his chest puffed out, really putting on a show. His nearly bullet-proof gelled hair gleamed under the dim streetlights. He was the most popular kid in our eighth-grade class, which made zero sense to me. I guess all a guy had to do to be cool in Ambler was play football and have massive nostrils. I'm serious. Blake's were huge. Probably stretched wide from years of picking.

He'd made my first few weeks of eighth grade miserable, mocking my every move and making sure everyone knew I wasn't worth befriending. He'd also gotten me in trouble with a bunch of my teachers, blaming me for all sorts of stuff. Anytime someone was talking, chucking wads of paper, or adding another pencil to the collection stuck into the ceiling tiles, he'd announce to the whole class that I'd done it. That led to a lot of "little chats" with teachers and several lunch detentions.

During history class, I'd overheard his plans for tonight. They were going ghost hunting in this old railroad museum. He'd made it sound scary, trying to prank his friends, acting like there were really ghosts here. I'd decided it was the perfect chance for payback. Blake was about to see a master prankster at work.

Lilly came next. She was wearing Blake's Eagles jacket. My face burned with jealous flames, lighting each of my freckles on fire. She shivered, her arms wrapped tightly around her body. Blue moonlight danced in her auburn hair. I was sorry she'd be a part of this, but when the perfect prank revealed itself in my mind, there was no backing out.

Too bad. Because she was the only thing about Ambler I liked.

Austin came last. He was an oafy kid who played center on the school's football team. His arms reminded me of a gorilla's, long and bulky with patches of dark hair growing in randomly, like some of his genes had gone through puberty and some decided they would get around to it later. His voice was like that, too. Usually deep, but often interrupted by high-pitched cracks.

Blake's was the first voice I heard. "That new guy needs a beating. Thinking he's all cool. When I see him tomorrow. . . ."

"His name's Caleb, and you should give him a break."

Wow. Some support from Austin? That was unexpected.

"Shut up. Just get us in." Blake commanded. "It's

freezing out here."

"Yeah, I've got the key here somewhere." Austin dug through his pockets and pulled out a jangly key ring. His breath came out in a cloud of cold as he searched for the right one.

Tick, tick, tick, tick. . . .

Could they hear it too? Was everyone in Ambler just used to it?

"We shouldn't be here," Lilly said. "Let's just go."

"Oh, come on, Lilly. Where's your sense of adventure? Don't you want to see a ghost?"

"You're not funny, Blake."

"Really." Austin thumbed through the thousands of keys. "This place is haunted."

Haunted? Was he serious? These Ambler kids were so superstitious.

"Don't you know the story of Matthew Bradford?" Austin examined one key in the moonlight.

Lilly shivered. "I don't like that story."

"You know it, right Blake?"

"Yeah, but tell it again, anyway. We're about to go into the place where he died."

Austin shoved the key into the padlock. "So, there was this kid named Matthew Bradford. . . ."

"Speed it up, dude. It's freezing out here. Come on!" Blake said.

CLACK.

"Got it. Let's go." Austin pushed the door open. It creaked in protest. Their shadowy bodies slipped into the doorway. Lilly waited behind. A hand reached out of the doorway and grabbed onto her arm.

"Don't worry. I'll be right here for you," Blake said.

Ugh. Barf.

I stood and wiped my nose on my sleeve. The balloon bobbed up behind me as I ran silently toward the door. Blake had left it open just a crack. I peered inside. The main hallway was empty. Blake and his ghost-hunter buddies must've moved on already.

Tick, tick, tick, tick. . . .

It was louder than before. The obnoxious clock must've been inside after all.

The museum stank of rotting wood. Pale moonlight flooded into the dark entryway from a window near the door. The space was large, with much of it occupied by an old train engine shimmering in the middle of the floor, its smokestack looming above me. An antique wooden desk sat behind it, shadowy picture frames lining the walls. A hallway stood on either side of the desk, set up to funnel proud residents around the oh-so-interesting museum.

I pulled my flashlight out of my backpack. I needed to be quick.

"So Bradford came here two years ago." Austin's voice came from down the hall to my right. "He snuck in and didn't come out for a whole day. When he finally did, there was something wrong with him. He went back to his house and started talking all crazy. He said terrible stuff to his mom and threatened to kill his little sister."

Geez. What was wrong with the people in this town?

Austin kept going. "His mom called the police because of the stuff he'd said. Really twisted stuff. Before the cops could get there, he disappeared."

Tick, tick, tick, tick. . . .

That sound was driving me crazy. I took off my backpack and scanned the room. Dusty cardboard boxes were stacked against the walls beneath the tarp-covered display cases. Still no sign of a clock.

"That night, the police answered an emergency call. When they got to the crime scene, they found Bradford's bike smashed through a neighbor's window. No one was hurt, but they were really scared. Bradford got cut up pretty bad by the glass, so the police followed his trail of blood. Then they found him. He was back in the Railroad Museum, curled up on the floor of this very room, and he was dead."

The floor creaked beneath my foot. I stopped dead in my tracks.

"Shhh. Did you hear that?" Austin asked.

"I swear if you guys are trying to scare me, I'll spray both of you with my can of mace," Lilly said.

Blake pushed out a forced laugh. "It's nothing. Stop being such babies."

I let out a breath. Close call.

"I want to go home," Lilly said. "Something's not right here."

"I feel it, too. A dark presence." Austin's voice cracked.

"I can't believe you two," Blake snorted. "I thought you wanted to come here to see a ghost. Now you're scared of some stupid ghost story?"

"It's not just a story," Lilly said. "It's real. I knew Matthew."

Maybe Lilly was just like the rest of them. Superstitious. Mind messed up from all this small-town nonsense and that endless ticking.

"Why don't we check out a different room?" Austin suggested.

They trudged out of the first room and down the dark hallway.

So. That room held more power over this little group of ghost hunters than any other. Relocating would take my prank from pretty good to colossal.

A risk. But totally worth it.

I tiptoed through the hallway and pressed my back

against a wall. Around the corner, a flashlight beam blazed across the floor in front of my shoes.

"I heard something again," Lilly whispered.

"You two are so pathetic," Blake said. "Come on. I'll show you the room where the hot chick on YouTube said she felt the most psychic energy."

The flashlight beam whipped away and disappeared through a doorway. I exhaled slowly and dashed toward the room where that Bradford kid had supposedly died.

There were no windows in the room, so the darkness was thick. Blackness surrounded me, smokelike, filling my lungs.

Tick, tick, tick, tick. . . .

Creeeak.

Cold sweat broke out on my forehead. I recognized that sound. Too high-pitched to be the floorboards. Metal and rubber.

Creeeak.

I was freaking out. I'd let Austin and his ghost stories get to me.

I ignored the darkness and plunged into the room, shining my flashlight beam all around. The walls were lined with stacks of wooden crates and some dust-caked glass cases. Larger objects were covered with splotchy canvas sheets.

An old dingy chest sat in a corner. The exterior was

made of carefully carved wood, leather straps bolted into the grain. A keyhole sat just under the lid, like a prop from an old pirate movie.

It was perfect. Exactly what I needed.

Tick, tick, tick, tick. . . .

The chest wasn't locked. I heaved the thick lid open. Red velvet shone under my flashlight beam. The smell reminded me of my dad's closet where I used to hide when I was a kid. All of his hangers were made from cedar because he said it kept the moths away.

I pushed all thoughts of my dad from my mind. I had work to do.

Inside the chest, I found an old candlestick, some dusty books, and finally, what appeared to be the source of the ticking.

A gold watch.

It was one of those old-style pocket watches that rich people always wore in movies, the kind with the metal cover that flips open when you press the button. How was it so loud that I could hear it outside?

It looked cool, but there was something more to it. Something that made me want to pick it up. Something that almost begged me to put that watch in my pocket.

I was no thief. I forced the idea from my mind. What was wrong with me? I had a job to do. Time to do it!

I tucked the ribbon of the balloon under the stack of books. Step one complete.

Next, I pulled a thin white bed sheet out of my backpack and draped it carefully over the balloon. It bobbed down under the weight but slowly drifted back up. Step two, done and working fine.

Step three: The finishing touches. I reached under the floating sheet and stood my flashlight on its end. Finally, I added pre-cut facial features to my homemade ghost.

Awesome! This was gonna be great.

I pushed my creation down into the chest and dropped the lid shut.

Footsteps. They were coming.

I'd originally planned to be in the entryway. Escape would be easy. Bolt for the front door when the prank was complete. This space gave me nowhere to go, but it would have to do. The risk was worth it to make my simple prank into a true masterpiece.

"So, see any ghosts?" Blake asked.

"Let's just get out of here," Lilly said.

"Oh, come on. Lighten up."

There was no way they were coming back into this room without a little motivation. For my prank to work, the chest had to become both the lure and the trap. I wedged my back against the wall into the shadows. The group was coming toward the doorway. This was it.

THUNK!

I kicked the crate in front of me. The footsteps stopped at the doorway.

"What was that?" Lilly whispered.

"Probably nothing," said Austin.

"Ahhhhhooohhhhhhhhhhh," I moaned.

The group went silent.

"Let's get out of here."

"Yeah, Lilly's right. I'm definitely feeling a weird aura or something," Austin said.

"Oh come on, guys." Blake laughed. "We came here to see a ghost. Let's see a ghost."

"Blake, I don't—," Lilly began.

"Come on," Blake said.

With my head peeking over a tarp-covered mound in the middle of the room, I watched as Blake slipped his hand into hers. I wanted to puke. Slowly, the group entered the room, walking toward me.

I needed to direct the group to the chest, but how? My leg was falling asleep, numbing prickles running through my calf muscle. I shifted my weight. Loose change jingled in my pocket.

Of course!I fished out a penny and tossed it at the chest. It hit with a clink and skittered to the floor. Blake leaped backward. I tried not to laugh.

"What was that?" Blake's voice cracked.

"I thought you weren't afraid," said Lilly.

"I'm not. It's just that, well, that was weird."

"Prove it. The sound came from over there. Go check it out." Now Lilly was having fun at Blake's expense. She scored another point in my book.

"I. . . uh. . . fine. I'm not scared." Blake strode forward, his chest puffed out to prove his manliness. I had to bite my tongue to keep from laughing.

I threw another penny. Blake jumped back as it rattled to the floor.

"What's going on here?" Blake's usual arrogance was completely washed away.

"I think the noise is coming from that chest." Lilly pointed right at it.

"I wouldn't open it. There's a real bad vibe coming from over there." Austin scratched his head. What a simple-minded boy he was.

"You guys are so childish." Blake regained his typical jerkiness, and, with those words, he threw the chest wide open.

My ghost rose out of the chest, glowing pale yellow against the deep purple shadows on the walls. Blake took one look into its soulless black eyes and gasped. All the ghost hunters went pale. Lilly screamed and stumbled toward the door. Austin tried to run, which led to an entanglement of limbs and a hard landing on the floor. Blake belted out a scream that hit soprano level.

I burst out laughing.

"Don't hurt us," Blake shouted. I doubled over. This was too good. I wished I'd thought to switch on my phone's video camera. Precious moments.

As I chortled in a heap on the floor, a spot of light landed on me. I looked up and saw Austin, his face covered in a dangerous glare.

"It's not real," Austin said. "It's a trick."

"It's a what?" Blake screamed.

"A trick. A fake," Austin said.

I tried to run, but Austin had me by the back of my shirt. In seconds, Blake was in my face.

"You think that's funny, punk?"

"Yeah. Yes, I do," I answered, still laughing.

Blake punched me, right in the face.

As I fell to the ground, it didn't seem so funny anymore.

CHAPTER

I was alone.

I sat in a ring of light in an empty room. The walls oozed blackness, like fresh asphalt. Cold prickles ran up my arms and legs, and then they went numb. I tried to stand, but I couldn't.

Creeeeeak.

The black stuff bubbled out of the wall in front of me, sliding down to the floor like a slug. It slopped into a pile, forming feet and legs. It only took seconds. Shoulders. A head.

A man in a wheelchair.

Creeeeeeak.

The squeal of metal and rubber. The man rolled closer, his breaths raspy and labored. My heart raced. My stomach cramped.

I couldn't move.

Creeeeeeak.

I knew who he was. I tried to close my eyes, but they wouldn't respond. I tried to stand again, but none of my limbs would obey. The shadow wheeled closer, the chair moving on its own.

Creeeeeeeak.

My father, or what once was my father, stared dully at me through dead eyes. His body was a heap of skin, a husk, planted in the wheelchair. His piercing blue eyes had gone out like an old light bulb, but they were open and they were fixed on me. His lips bulged and sagged. Living, but lifeless.

"Is that what you want, Caleb?" His voice came clearly, even though his mouth didn't move.

My heart pounded against my ribcage. What I wanted was to run, or at least look away. But I was frozen, my eyes glued open, focused on him.

"Is this what you wanted?"

Tears burned my eyes. I couldn't move my arms to wipe them away. He rolled closer.

Tick, tick, tick, tick. . . .

In a flash of light, he was gone. In his place, a golden orb hung in the air, blurry, like I was looking at it through a fogged window.

Tick, tick, tick, tick. . . .

Was that... it? That watch from the old museum?

A thick, grey mist dripped down the walls. It swirled around the golden orb. A tingling sensation ran up my arms and legs. I could move them again. I stood, carefully, holding my arms out from my sides to make sure I didn't fall. The vapors coiled together in mid-air in front of me, forming into the face of a man. His body dripped out beneath him.

He was older and very thin. The light blue suit he was wearing looked very expensive, but also like it was made centuries ago. The wrinkles around his small black eyes creased as he examined me. A smile spread across his thin lips.

The mist behind him formed into other shapes. People. Children. He was surrounded by at least twenty shadows, clothed in old-fashioned suits and dresses. Some were my age while others were much younger. The man reached his hand into his suit coat. I stepped forward in anticipation.

He had it. That watch. It shone gold against his gray body. The cover was engraved with a picture of a locomotive, the watch face concealed. I'd almost taken that watch. Why didn't I? It was the most beautiful thing I'd ever seen.

Although it made no sense, somehow I knew that watch was the answer to all my problems. If I could just touch it. Keep it.

The man held it out to me. It swung back and forth on its gold chain as I moved closer. The air around me became thick like cement, slowing me down as I approached the dangling gold. I reached for it, gravity fighting me back.

Just as my fingers were inches away from wrapping around the sleek body of that watch, the man slipped it back into his suit coat pocket.

I charged at him. He couldn't leave.

His body faded, almost transparent. I could see that watch, beating like a heart, through his suit coat. I reached for it again, but his body dissolved into a hissing black puddle. The group of children evaporated into pools of silvery water. The puddles seeped into the floor and disappeared without a trace.

I dropped to my knees. They couldn't leave. I had to go with them.

I needed that watch!

I tried to shout after them, beg them to stay. My jaw loosened, like it had been welded shut. My voice croaked out unintelligibly. A blast of orange light cut through the haze. I shielded my eyes.

"Come on, Caleb!"

I blinked and sat up in my creaky bed. I was in my room, but there were no dark mists or old men. Just my mom flicking the light switch on and off like she usually does when I don't respond to her first and second wake-up calls in the morning.

"Get up! You still have to go to school today," my mom said from the doorway, her finger still on the light switch. Raindrops pelted my window, obscuring the gloomy sky outside. There was no way I was going anywhere.

"I can't go. Too much emotional trauma last night."

"You will go, young man, and you will apologize." She waved a fingertip at me.

"Mom, I'm not apologizing. Those guys are jerks. They deserved what they got."

"I think you deserved what you got, too." She planted one hand on her hip and shook her head. "That eye of yours doesn't look any better. Put some ice on it before you leave."

"I'm not going to school, Mom."

"Get up, NOW!"

"Fine," I grumbled. I sat up and rubbed my eyes. "Ouch!"

Even barely touching my eye hurt like crazy. Blake had gotten me pretty good. Despite my shiner, the memory of Blake's face when he had met my ghost made it all worth it.

I kicked the blankets off of my feet and stumbled to the bathroom to examine the damage. My eye was surrounded by a crimson-splotched purple ring. It looked a lot worse than it had last night.

When my mom had shown up to get me, I told her the truth about what I'd done. She would've found out anyway, and I was kinda proud of my prank despite its tragic ending. So, I told her everything and she came unglued.

I splashed water on my face and looked into my own eyes. My brown hair was flattened on one side and standing straight up on the other. I almost laughed at my reflection, but I couldn't. There was a lingering feeling of dread, a cold shadow in my heart.

I remembered the dream.

And the watch.

CHAPTER

A train whistle moaned in the distance. I slipped into the car and tossed my backpack into the backseat. Mom didn't say a word.

We thumped over the cracked road and passed an old, rotted-wood light post. In parts of L.A., you had to look straight up to see the sky because of all of the buildings. Why were there so many buildings? Simple. People wanted to live there.

In Ambler, the sky seemed to go on forever.

"I think it's important for you to make some friends here," Mom said out of nowhere.

"Why? We're not staying. Please, Mom, let's just go home."

"We've been through this, Caleb," she answered without looking at me. "Aunt Kelsey was nice enough to let us live in her rental while we get settled in. We need this right now. We needed to get away. To start over."

I gritted my teeth.

Old brick buildings crumbled like sand on either side of the road. Even the street signs looked like they were from another time. I almost expected to see a friendly milkman waving to me as we whizzed by.

"Maybe tomorrow we can go out to get you a new jacket and then check out that castle up on the hill." She wouldn't look at me. Her eyes were glued on the road ahead.

"No thanks."

She kept trying. "Did you know that a movie was filmed in the castle in the sixties?"

"Did you know that the guy who built that castle invented asbestos?" I countered.

"It won't kill you to see the town, Caleb."

"It might, Mom. Asbestos."

Her hands trembled on the steering wheel.

"You need to get used to being here. You know we couldn't afford to live in Los Angeles anymore, and I need to be around family. Your aunt Kelsey and uncle Ron have been so helpful. I couldn't stay in that house anymore. Not after what happened. I couldn't face our old life and our old friends." She wiped a tear from her eye and clenched her quivering lips. "We're not going back."

I didn't respond.

"You need to go see him," she said, staring at the road ahead.

I shook my head. I couldn't believe she'd bring this up. "No, I don't."

"Caleb, he wants to see you."

I saw him in my mind. Trapped in that wheelchair. Eyes staring blankly.

"Did he tell you that?"

"Caleb–"

"Did he open his mouth and say that to you? If not, how do you know he wants to see me?"

"Caleb, he's your father. He still wants to see you."

"No."

Mom went silent. Those bags under her eyes. It was like they grew four times bigger. I didn't mean to hurt her, but I wasn't going along with it. Ever since we'd arrived she'd tried to lure me out with Ambler sight-seeing, but I wasn't falling for it. I didn't care about the attractions in this stupid place. I just wanted to go back home. I wanted our old life back.

Silence until we reached the school. The brakes whined as the sedan shimmied to a stop.

Mom took a deep breath, still fighting back tears. I couldn't stay mad at her. She tried so hard to be strong for me, but I knew her life was broken into pieces on the night of the accident too. I wouldn't go see my dad, but I could at least try to make her feel a little bit better.

"I'm sorry, Mom."

Her lower lip trembled. "I know, honey. This has been really hard on both of us."

"See you after school." I leaned across the seat to give her a hug. She held on for a minute then pushed me away.

"Now get your butt to class and make some friends," she said, wiping another tear from her eye.

I forced my most convincing smile. "You bet."

The school stood before me, a two-story brown brick monster. Crowds of kids flooded into the glass double doors. Why were they in such a hurry to get inside?

The thought hit me hard. I didn't need to go. I could just walk away. No one would notice anyway.

I could wander down to the museum, grab that old watch. . . .

Blake appeared out of nowhere, his arms crossed over his chest, his mouth curled in a snarl. He'd been waiting for me. I glanced back toward the parking lot. Mom's car was gone. Blake was faster and stronger than me. Fight or flight, I lose.

Of course, he'd already punched me. What else could he do?

"You think you're pretty funny, don't you?" Blake said. The crowd of students opened up into an arena of

33

nosy onlookers excited to watch me get my face pounded in. Blake stood in front of me, like an angry rhino
with steel-gelled hair.

"Yeah. I'm funny," I answered. He puffed out a
misty breath.

"You're so lucky Lilly pulled me away. I would've
broken your bones."

"You might've already. My poor bones. Shattered by
all your high-pitched screaming."

Some kids giggled at my comeback. Most just stared
at me like I was crazy. I was really asking for it.

Blake glared at the crowd and then at me. "I should
drop you right here."

This all would've seemed like the end of the world
back in L.A., but my world had already ended. Blake
didn't scare me.

"Go right ahead."

His hands curled into fists. He charged.

"Probably shouldn't do that, Blake," said a deep
voice behind me.

Blake skidded to a halt. "Austin?"

"Don't you all have to get to your classes?" Austin
said to our audience, "You're gonna be late."

The crowd started to break formation, their eyes
still glued to Blake to see what he was going to do. I
guess the pressure was too much for him. Blake stomped

34

toward me. Austin stood between us.

"Walk away, Austin. You know he deserves it. The little punk!"

"He does deserve it, but you won't be playing in Saturday's game if you do anything to him. In fact, I'm hoping Caleb will keep his mouth shut about his black eye so Coach and the principal don't find out who gave it to him."

Blake glared at me and then back to Austin. His fists clenched and unclenched as he ground his teeth together. Finally, his shoulders slumped. He stepped in closer. Right in my face.

"You say a word to anyone about what happened last night and you're dead."

I stared right back at him. "The only thing that's deadly about you is your breath."

His face lit up red. For a second, I was sure he was going to hit me again. Why was I egging him on? What was wrong with me? He'd already given me a black eye. Did I secretly want a matching set?

"Stay away from me. You hear me?" Blake stormed off toward the building, pushed the glass doors open, and disappeared inside. The die-hard fight fans wandered away too, disappointed the main event had been canceled.

"You okay?" Austin asked.

"What do you want?" I started toward the school doors.

He followed behind me. "Man, I thought you'd be a lot more grateful. I got Blake to leave you alone."

"Well, he's your friend, so you're just doing your best to keep him out of trouble."

"Not really." His massive hand grabbed onto my shoulder. "I need to ask you something. Something serious."

I rolled my eyes and turned around. "Fine. What?"

"Was there anything in that old chest?"

"You mean besides a ghost?"

"Yes, I mean besides *your* ghost." Austin's eyes focused on me like a hunter aiming a rifle.

"Why?" I felt strangely protective of the watch. I didn't want him to know about it. What if he took it? He couldn't have it. It was mine.

His voice cracked. "I have my reasons."

Austin was pretty intense about this. What was up with that? He had keys to the place. If he wanted to know what was in that chest, why didn't he just go back and find out?

No. I didn't want him to find out.

"Nothing much. Some dingy old books and a candlestick, I think. I can't remember anything else."

His eyes narrowed on me. "So, nothing out of the

ordinary?"

"I don't know. Is that ordinary?"

"That's a good question." He tilted his head back and stared down a patch of storm clouds hovering above us.

Okay, weird-o."Is that all you wanted?"

"Yeah, I think so. See you in history." Austin walked toward the school. I decided my first impression of him was correct. Idiot. Weird idiot. Why would he care what was in that chest?

A second theory popped into my mind. Maybe he was smarter than I thought? Maybe he was playing dumb to get me back. That might be it. He might try to get me interested by being mysterious and then lure me back to the museum to scare me. That would be a pretty good plan.

I watched him bob along toward the school, his long arms swinging widely with each step.

His backpack slid off of his shoulder. It must have been unzipped because all of his books flopped out on the wet school lawn followed by the contents of his sack lunch.

"Aw crap!" he hollered. Some other students laughed. I brushed past him and walked through the doors into the school.

Nope. No brilliant plan. Austin was just an idiot.

CHAPTER

The day went by slowly. I did have a lot more people talking to me. Unfortunately, they were only asking about my eye, and I felt honor-bound not to tell them what really happened. Not so much for Blake's sake, but for Austin's. It was kinda cool of him to get Blake to leave me alone, no matter what his reasons were for doing it.

At lunch, I looked for Lilly as I sat at a table by myself. Even sixth and seventh graders wouldn't sit by me just to make sure they didn't end up on Blake's radar. At least I had time to think.

Lilly walked through the cafeteria doors. She'd braided her hair, strands of orange and red interwoven like rays of sunshine. She chatted with two other girls when she came in. Blake crept up behind her.

"Caleb." I jumped in my seat and turned back to

the table. Austin and some sixth-grade girl were directly across from me. I hadn't noticed them sit down at all.

"Did we scare you?" Austin smirked.

"Uh, yeah. A little. Does this mean we're even?"

The little girl ran her fingers through her straight brown hair. Her smile was nearly identical to Austin's. "Instead of just staring, maybe you should go talk to her."

"What?"

"Lilly. You know."

"Who's this?" I asked Austin.

Austin wrapped his extra-long arm around her. "Caleb, meet my little sister, Hillary."

Hillary smiled wide at the mention of her name. "Austin told me about your prank. That was pretty good."

"Oh. Thanks." Surprising how any compliment felt good at this point.

She continued. "But seriously. Just go talk to Lilly. Talking to her is better than just staring. Staring is creepy."

Social advice from a sixth grader. As if my life could get any worse. Still, she was actually having a conversation with me, so I figured I'd humor her.

"Thanks for the tip," I said. "Maybe I'll talk to her in class."

"Sounds good," Austin said. "For now, I want to ask

you some questions."

"Go ahead."

He folded his hands and leaned closer. "Are you sure there wasn't something odd in that chest?"

"Are you serious? You already asked me about this."

He leaned in even closer, eyes wide. "I know there was something else in there. Something that was giving off evil energy."

"Evil energy? Ummmmm... okay?" I took a bite of my apple.

"I want to go back tonight to check it out." Austin continued. "There was a really bad vibe in that room."

"You felt a vibe?"

"Yeah, didn't you?"

Hillary watched our conversation like a tennis match, her wide brown eyes darting between us.

The watch appeared in my mind. Austin didn't know about it. But he was going back? He might find it.

"No, I didn't feel anything."

"Of course you didn't," Hillary said. "Austin is more sensitive to these kinds of things than normal people."

Normal people?

I had to ask a follow-up question. "Are you saying he's psychic or something?"

"No, he's just sensitive. He can feel paranormal presences."

Paranormal presences?

"Hillary," Austin interrupted. She huffed and crossed her arms.

"Are you talking about ghosts?" I asked.

Austin cleared his throat. "I know you don't believe in that stuff, Caleb. Don't worry about it, okay?"

Austin stared at the table, like he was embarrassed by what his sister had told me. His delusions about sensing the undead weren't my biggest concern.

The watch was.

"Are you going back into the museum?"

"Probably. Come on, Hillary." They stood up to go.

"Wait." The word came out before I'd even thought it. I didn't want them to go. It'd been nice having someone to talk to. But I needed to play it cool. "Tell me more about the museum. I heard you telling Blake and Lilly a story about some kid dying in there."

Austin sat back down.

"What do you know about Ambler, Caleb?" He stared at me, super-serious.

I shook my head. "Not much."

"Do you even know how the town got its name?"

"I saw a plaque on the side of the museum. Said it was in honor of Mary Ambler. I'm guessing she has something to do with it."

Hillary rolled her eyes. "Wow. Good guess."

"Yeah. Do you know who she was?"

"Nope."

"So, you've never heard about the train crash?" Austin's eyes were wide, like he couldn't believe it.

"Everyone knows about that," Hillary said.

I'd tried to learn as little about this place as possible, actively made sure I wouldn't get too cozy. I couldn't let my mom see any signs of me giving up on going home.

But now, I genuinely wanted to know.

"Well, fill me in."

Austin stretched his arms above his head, and then took a deep breath, like telling the story was some kind of athletic event. "So, in 1856, there was this train heading to a church picnic. Bunch of kids from all over the nearby areas on it. Problem was, they left the station late. There was another train. . . ."

I waved my hand to stop him. "Wait. So, these two trains crashed? How? They weren't on different tracks?"

"No," Hillary said, her eyes just as focused and serious and Austin's. "Back then trains ran on the same tracks. If the train had left on time, it would've hit a junction way before the other train showed up. But it didn't."

"So, the trains collided head on." Austin smashed his hands together to demonstrate, "And the boilers in both trains exploded. So many people died."

"And then Mary Ambler came running to the rescue," Hillary said. "She heard the explosion and made bandages and stretchers out of anything she could find. She saved so many lives that our borough changed its name to Ambler."

I was putting the pieces together. "So, you believe that the railroad museum is haunted by the ghosts of the people in the train accident? Do you think they killed that Bradford kid?"

Austin smiled. "I'm not sure what I think. All I know is there's a dark feeling in there. Especially in that one room. Especially around that chest."

"Hi, Caleb." I jumped. Lilly had walked up behind me and I hadn't even noticed.

"Oh, uh. . . hi." I could barely string words together. She was talking to me.

"I want to show you something." She held out her hand. A diamond earring sat in her palm, its facets sparkling in the light cast from the cafeteria's windows.

"What's wrong with this?" she demanded.

My brain was on lockdown, my pulse pounding in my head. She stood there, only a foot or two away from me, her hand on her hip, waiting for an answer. I'd always hoped she'd talk to me. Now she was, and I was totally blowing it. I blurted the only thing my brain would give me.

"Uh, I don't know. It's very pretty."

Her lips cinched together. "It *is* very pretty. But, there's only one. There are supposed to be two, Caleb."

"Oh yeah. Two. That's right." What in the world was she talking about? I glanced back at Austin and Hillary for help. Their faces were red, on the verge of exploding with laughter.

Thanks, guys.

"Do you know the last time I saw the other one?" Lilly demanded.

I tried to force myself to look at her, but failed and ended up staring at my apple. "Uh, no."

"It was in my ear when I went into the museum last night, but it wasn't when I came out."

Oh. She lost it in the museum. She was blaming me.

"I . . . uh, I'm really sorry about that. I didn't really want to scare you. I just wanted to scare Blake."

"You didn't scare me that much, Caleb. Your little ghost trick was a shock at first, but only someone really gullible would've been scared of it for more than two seconds."

"Blake was scared of it for more than two seconds," I said. Lilly slipped a quick smile, but then she reverted to being mad at me again.

I glanced over her shoulder and found Blake,

44

glaring at me from across the cafeteria, angrily stuffing his mouth full of cafeteria creamed corn.

"To be honest, I didn't even want to go to that museum in the first place. You guys both owe me." Now she was staring Austin down.

"What about Blake? He was the one who convinced you." Austin rubbed his chin.

"True. But I don't want Blake coming with us tonight."

"What're you talking about?" Austin asked.

"I need to find my earring. It probably fell off when Caleb scared us, so we're all going back to the museum tonight so you both can help me find it."

"Okay, okay." Austin nodded at her. "But why don't you want Blake to come?"

Lilly smirked. "He'd be trying to find ways to get back at Caleb all night. I don't have time for that. I want to get my earring and get out."

There was something in her voice that told me she was lying. An urgency. An anger. A need that was about more than just recovering her earring. Why couldn't Austin go get it alone? Or me and Austin? If she didn't want to be in the museum before, why did she seem so eager to go now?

Did she know about the watch?

My fist clenched around my apple, knuckles going

white.

Did she want it too?

"Meet us at my house at seven o'clock tonight." Austin pulled out his phone. "Give me your number and I'll text you my address."

"Don't bring your stupid little ghost friend this time," said Lilly.

"But he gets lonely."

Lilly gave a short laugh and shook her head before she walked off. Austin smacked me on the shoulder as the bell rang.

"Guess I'll see you tonight."

"I'm coming this time!" Hillary demanded.

"No way, Hill. There's something in there. Something dark."

"Yep. And I get to go or I'll tell Mom and Dad about how you dented the car fender when you were shooting hoops." She smiled at me. "They still think it was a hit and run."

Austin rubbed his forehead in defeat. "Ugghh. Fine. You win. We'll all go." Austin shoved his sandwich into his mouth. The whole thing at once. He and Hillary stood up to go.

"See you tonight, Caleb," Austin said, his mouth still full.

"Bye." Hillary waved her lunch box at me. They

disappeared into the crowd as I chucked my apple into a massive garbage can.

I was going back to the museum, back to the old chest, and this time, I wouldn't leave until I'd banished my nightmares. I wouldn't leave afraid.

I wouldn't leave without the watch.

CHAPTER

Mom picked me up after school like usual. Normally, she'd be wearing her work clothes, but she was dressed in blue jeans and a sweater.

I plopped into the passenger seat. "Don't you have to work?"

"David gave me the rest of the day off," she replied. This wasn't good. Family time.

I threw my backpack into the back of our dark blue Lexus. The car was one of the last reminders I had of where I'd come from. It was only a year or two old and the leather seats still smelled brand new.

Austin and Hillary walked by in the distance. He grinned and waved at me.

Mom glanced at them before pulling out of the parking lot. "Oh. That's nice. Is he a new friend?"

"Kind of." I shifted in my seat. "He's one of the

people I scared last night."

"The one that gave you that black eye?"

"No."

"You apologized?"

"Uh, yeah. Pretty much."

"Well, that's good. You see, if you treat people decently, you find out that they are decent people," Mom said, without taking her eyes off of the road.

Mom took a turn that led away from our house. I clenched my teeth, almost too afraid to ask. "Where are we going?"

"I scheduled another meeting with Dr. Ross."

My fists balled up. "What?"

"We're both going. We need this." Mom wouldn't look at me.

"I'm fine. I don't need therapy."

"Well, I do." Her face went red, eyes glistening. "I guess you'll just have to come along for the ride."

It would be pointless to argue with her, so I leaned my head back against the headrest and tried to calm down. Going in all pissed off would only make a stronger case to Dr. Ross that I wasn't coping well.

We came to a stoplight on Main Street. A sign bolted to a building lit up red against the darkening sky, vertical neon letters that spelled AMBLER. We sat in silence as a train whistle moaned in the distance.

For a moment, I wondered what the town had looked like in 1856. Where had the trains crashed? How far did Mary Ambler have to walk? What would she have thought about the red sign that glowed before me now, spelling out her name?

My thoughts ended abruptly as the car lurched forward, the signal reflecting green light on my mom's face. Her bottom lip trembled slightly. She was really hurting. Badly.

She would do anything for me and all I did was make her feel worse. The problem was I didn't know what to say to her. I wanted more than anything to make her smile again. Make her laugh. But I was empty inside. How could I make her feel better when I felt like crap? A tiny part of me was glad that we were on our way to Dr. Ross's office, for her sake. Maybe for mine, too, but I would never admit that.

The waiting room always smelled like cinnamon and body odor. The people waiting to see one of the therapists at the office were a mixed bag, some very proper, dressed in elegant clothes. Others were loud, over-friendly folks that wanted to start their session before they got in to see their doctor.

When we went in, the waiting room was empty except for an older man sitting in a cushy armchair. He nodded at me as I walked by.

Whatever, Weird-o.

After checking in, Mom dropped into an orange vinyl seat. I sat beside her, the cushion hissing out air as I settled into it.

Dr. Ross emerged from one of the dark wood doors that lined the back wall. He was a chunky, balding man with a broad smile and intimidating thick-rimmed glasses. "Hello, Arlene. Come on back."

Dr. Ross always wanted Mom to go in first to "check in." I knew that was code for "talk about Caleb behind his back."

My mom walked through the doorway with Dr. Ross. The heavy wooden door closed behind her. The secretary typed something on her computer, a rhythmic click-clacking of plastic keys against her fake fingernails. Other than that, the only sound was the buzzing of the lights above me.

I jumped. The old man was sitting right next to me.

I scooted as far from him in my seat as I could. His closeness made me uncomfortable. He nodded at me again to get my attention. What was wrong with this guy? I decided to get away from him and fast. He smiled at me and reached into his jacket.

His face changed. His shabby clothes became a suit, light blue with a solid silver tie. I recognized him. The old man from my dream.

He pulled his hand out of his coat. The veiny flesh trembled. A golden glow came through his skin, silhouetting the bones and tendons that wrapped around the object he clutched in his hand so tightly. He opened his fingers.

The watch.

I looked into his face, startled. He was smiling. His dull eyes glimmered with kindness, but my heart filled with a sense of dread. My blood ran cold as it pulsed through my body to the pace of my speeding heartbeat.

The watch.

Its casing was closed tightly, glowing like an ember. Gold essence drifted from it and absorbed into my body, warming me like a crackling campfire. Fear fled the golden vapors, leaving my chest empty and deflated. I felt only longing. Uncontrollable need. I wanted the watch.

I had to have it.

I lunged for it. The man held it out to me. He wanted me to take it. It was mine.

Then, he was gone. The watch was gone. I sat, bewildered, looking all around the room. What had just happened? Had anyone else seen the old man? Where was the watch?

"Caleb?" Dr. Ross emerged from his doorway.

I jumped in my seat.

He grinned. "We're ready for you."

I wiped the sweat beads from my forehead and stood. There was no one else in the waiting room. I was alone.

The secretary tapped the counter with her fingernails as I walked toward Doctor Ross. I turned around and gave the waiting room one last look.

"Did you lose something?" she asked.

Yeah. My mind, I thought as I followed Dr. Ross through the doorway.

We walked down the short hallway that led to a larger, heavier oak door. He twisted the door handle and beckoned me inside. He tucked himself into a burgundy leather armchair across from my mom.

Mom patted the cushion next to her on the fluffy white couch with a floral print. I walked to her, my limbs stiff, and sat down. Dr. Ross examined my face.

"Caleb? Is something wrong? You look like you've just seen a ghost."

I nodded absently. My mom smacked my knee. I jumped at the sudden contact.

"Wake up, Caleb. We pay this man by the hour."

"Sorry. Just sleepy, I guess," I said.

"That's okay, Caleb. Your mother and I were just talking about how this week has been for the two of you." He scooted forward in his chair.

Every time we met with Dr. Ross, he would wriggle in his seat and the resulting friction of his pants and the leather made funny fart sounds. Or maybe he was really farting and just blaming it on the chair. Either way, I was not allowed to laugh when this happened. I usually did, though. In return, I was gifted with fiery glares from my mom.

"So, things are better. I'm doing great. Can we go, now?" Mom shot me a warning look.

"Actually, Caleb, your mother thinks you've gotten worse."

"Worse?" So not just back-talk, but betrayal. Nice, Mom.

"Yes. She said that you haven't been in contact with any of your old friends. Why is that?"

"Yes, I have. I talk to them at least once a day," I said. Mom shook her head at Dr. Ross but didn't say a word.

"Although you need to separate yourself from your past, severing your old friendships completely is not a healthy way to make a transition," Dr. Ross said. My face flushed. I didn't know my mom was monitoring how often I talked to my old friends. Was she monitoring my bathroom usage too? What happened to my right to privacy?

"Is there any particular reason you've stopped

communicating with your friends from California?" Dr. Ross asked.

I didn't know what to say. I knew my friends didn't know what to say either. What do you say to someone like me? Someone who loses everything? I spared them the nuisance of having to try and never replied to their texts.

Dr. Ross noticed this line of questioning wasn't getting him anywhere, so he switched topics.

"It sounds like you've been in some trouble at school and that you haven't been doing well on your school work. Your mother informed me about your prank and how you earned your shiner there." Dr. Ross pointed to my bruised eye.

His over-friendly tone made me explode.

"Did she tell you about how they treat me at school? Did she tell you about the jerk who punched me? Did she tell you that it's this place that's making me crazy?"

"Caleb, this place is part of a very hard transition that your family had to make. The changes began with what happened to your father."

His words made me one million percent more angry. My hand burned from strangling the armrest of the fluffy couch. "This has nothing to do with my dad."

"I think it might. Please tell me more about how you're feeling in regards to your father."

I closed my eyes and tried to calm down. Getting mad made everything worse. But Dr. Ross's question was irritating, like a high-pitched buzzing in my ear. My feelings toward my father? The man who I looked up to? Loved? Now the man I saw in my nightmares? How did I feel about him?

The truth hit me. I didn't know how I felt about my father. I felt anger, stress, and afraid. Very afraid.

"I don't feel anything," I lied. Dr. Ross adjusted himself in his seat.

Prrbbbrrrttttt.

A really good one, but I wasn't in the mood for laughing. I sat still, my arms folded across my chest, refusing to look back at him.

"Do you feel responsible for what happened to him?"

My mom always said: *It's not your fault, Caleb.* I knew she didn't believe it, either.

"*Is that what you want, Caleb?*" His last words to me. What if I hadn't wanted anything? What if I'd have just wanted him to stay there with me? To stay home. Wouldn't everything be different?

How could I not feel responsible for what happened to him?

But I could never admit it to Dr. Ross.

"No," I answered.

"Caleb, I want to help you, but you'll need to give me something to work with. You need to let me know what's going on inside your head."

"What if I don't know what's going on inside my head?"

"I think you do know, but you don't want anyone else to know. I want to help, Caleb."

"I don't need any help, Dr. Ross, but thanks for offering."

He leaned in, still not giving up. "Everyone has feelings, Caleb. They're nothing to be ashamed of."

"I said I don't feel anything, okay?" My mom put her hand on my shoulder. I brushed it off. Dr. Ross lowered his face, his chins multiplying under his black goatee. He looked up at me again, still smiling.

"If you don't feel anything, then why won't you go and see him?" Dr. Ross asked.

Not this again.

"I don't know."

"Then you need to find out." He turned to my mother. "I want him to go visit his dad."

I leaned back on the sofa. "Not happening."

"You may have struck the nail on the head, Caleb. You may truly not know why you are so frightened of seeing your father. My guess is that seeing him may sort those emotions out for you. It won't be easy, but nothing worthwhile is easy."

"You make a ton of money at this job for sitting in a big chair and telling people what to do," I snapped. "That sounds easy."

Dr. Ross tilted his head, still examining me.

My mom wrapped her hand around my wrist. "Caleb, stop right there. You keep this up and you'll be grounded. No leaving the house except for school and no video games. Do you understand me?"

The Railroad Museum. The watch.

I was so close to losing my chance at getting the only thing that might help me with all of the anger, all of the fear. The watch that sat in the quiet darkness, waiting.

Waiting for me.

I sucked in a deep breath.

"I understand. Sorry."

Dr. Ross jumped on this opportunity. "Caleb, will you accompany your mother on her next trip to visit your father?"

"Yeah. Sure," I answered. I would've agreed to anything at that moment. I had to be able to go out tonight.

"Great." My mom sat up, her hands on her knees. "We'll go right after we're done here."

Panic set in. I wasn't actually going to see him. I was going to the museum. I would get the watch. Before

Austin. Before Lilly. Before anyone else.

"I don't want to go until Saturday." I pivoted toward her on the couch. "I need some time to prepare myself."

"I'm going to take you over there right now," Mom said.

I stared at Dr. Ross with pleading in my eyes.

"It's only a day, Arlene. I think it can wait." Dr. Ross folded his hands.

Mom sighed. "Fine."

"Caleb, you need to do this." He nodded at me. "Trust me, it's the only way you're going to really understand what you're feeling, the only way you'll be able to move forward."

"Yes sir," I said. "I'll go. I promise."

Deep inside, I knew the only place I was going was to the museum. After that, whatever. My problems would no longer mean anything after I had the watch.

If I had it, I had everything.

If I had it, I would never be afraid again.

CHAPTER 6

s that what you want, Caleb?" My dad said. He stood by the door, wearing his chocolate brown suit and solid gold tie.

"Yep. Rocky Road's my favorite." My mouth moved and the words came out, even though inside I wanted it all to stop. I wanted to tell him to forget it. Just stay home.

Stay home.

"What the birthday boy wants, the birthday boy gets," Mom said. Dad winked at my mom. She smiled at him as he stepped out the front door of our condo.

And then I was there, even though I wasn't. I could see it all, like I was watching it from the sky. I saw everything. Why would my brain do that to me? Why would it create images of something I would never want to see and then force me to watch it over and over again?

The first thing I recognized was his car. Sleek, silver. My dad drove down a mostly empty street, the setting sun reflecting in his windshield. He sang along to his favorite song, "*I Saw Her Standing There*" by the Beatles.

He was an accountant for a firm that worked with some of the big movie companies, helping them finance their films. His eyes were sharp, pale blue, constantly calculating numbers as he drove and sang. He was a multitasker; a self-made man. He could do anything.

But he didn't stop at the red light.

A big rig slammed into the driver's side. Dad's car crumpled like an aluminum can. His fancy suit was red with blood. His eyes closed. I wished I could close my eyes, but I couldn't. I had to watch. I had no choice.

Sirens blared. The wreckage of the car moved, shifted. Shreds of tire rubber coiled around twisted metal trim. The rest of the car melted away from the driver's seat.

All that was left was a wheelchair. And a man in the wheelchair. My dad.

His chest heaved up and down. His eyes flicked open, but there was no music, no calculation. All that was left was pale blue and dead.

In a flash, I was in a room with him, a dark room. I couldn't move my head. I couldn't close my eyes. I could only stare into the pale blue eyes where my father once was.

I woke up with a start, sweating. My pulse raced as I stood up from my bed and rubbed my forehead. I tried to dislodge the images left over from the dream.

I'd fallen asleep after the appointment. Sounds and smells of sizzling meat and soy sauce drifted through my bedroom door. Dinner was almost ready.

I wasn't hungry.

And I wasn't going to see my dad.

I stumbled down the stairs, pushing my hair out of my eyes. Mom dropped chopped vegetables into the steaming wok.

"You okay?" She drizzled in some sesame oil. I rubbed my clammy forehead.

"Yeah, fine."

"Sit down. It'll be ready in a minute."

Mom seemed extra cheery. Her face was plastered with her wide, plastic smile. Because I'd told her I would go see Dad. I had to catch my breath again. The realization hit me harder than Blake had. I would be in that room, trapped with him.

My hands were still shaking from the dream. I couldn't take it anymore.

I needed a way out.

I needed the watch. Just like in the waiting room,

when the watch had chased away my terror. If I had it, there'd be no more nightmares. No more staring into my father's dull eyes. No more being trapped in my own fear. The watch was the key to my freedom.

"I'm not really hungry."

Mom laughed. "*You* aren't hungry? Should I call a doctor?"

"That's super funny, Mom."

I walked toward the front door.

"Where are you going?"

"To hang out with some friends."

"I don't think so. Sit down and eat your dinner." Her plastic smile had crumbled.

"Oh come on, Mom. There's a football game and some of the guys invited me to come."

"I thought you hated football." She wasn't buying it.

"Well, you thought wrong." I twisted the doorknob.

Mom turned off the stove. "Fine. But don't schedule anything for tomorrow."

"I might be busy tomorrow." I slipped into my jacket.

She turned to me, eyes bloodshot. "You'll be busy going to visit your father with me."

"Yeah. Sure." Anything to appease her.

She slammed down the spatula. "Stop lying to me! Stop lying to yourself!"

I spun around, face red. "Fine, Mom. Fine. You're right. I don't want to go see him. There. That's the truth. I don't want to."

"Why not, Caleb? Why would you abandon your father?"

"I'm not abandoning him. He's not even there anymore."

"That's not true, Caleb. You need to go see him. You can't run away from what happened anymore. You need to face reality."

"I need to face reality? Come on, Mom. Why do you want to go see him? Does it make you feel better? When you sit and stare back into his dead eyes do you think he even knows you're there?"

Mom was breaking. Her red face, her bleary eyes. Normally I would've stopped. I swear I would have.

I was obsessed. I only wanted one thing. It was like the golden glow of the watch had actually entered my bloodstream. I would do anything to get it.

Anything.

"How long until you realize he's gone?" I shouted. "How long until you accept that he's dead?"

My mom sobbed. She buried her face in her hands as I twisted the doorknob and pushed open the creaky door.

"Caleb," she said through tears. I refused to look at her. "I love you. Never forget that. He loves you, too."

I slammed the door before she could say another word.

CHAPTER

It was a long walk to Austin's but I didn't care. The cold air felt good on my face. I needed time away. Especially from my mom. She couldn't force me to see him.

My stomach churned with guilt. The stuff that was always there, plus a little extra for what I'd said to my mom. But she deserved it, right? Why wouldn't she get off my back?

I pushed all of that from my head. None of it mattered. It was all in the past.

Every footstep brought me closer to the watch. After I had it, I was sure I'd figure all of this out. It would take my fear away. Suck it right out of me.

Austin lived in an apartment complex. The gated pool shimmered in the rising moonlight as I sprinted up the steps to his door. I knocked. A tall woman with brown hair tied up into a ponytail whipped the door open. A smile stretched completely across her face as she waved both arms at me, motioning for me to come in.

"You must be Caleb. We're just finishing dinner. Would you like to join us?" Her arms flailed around, like a marionette controlled by a drunk guy. I waited on the doormat to avoid being accidentally slapped.

"No thanks."

"Well, join us anyway. We always like to get to know Austin's friends." She beckoned me inside and then slammed the door shut behind me.

"No need to be shy. Make yourself at home," she said as she breezed by me.

I followed her through the cluttered front room. The smell of basil, tomato sauce, and sourdough bread drifted into my nostrils. My stomach rumbled.

"I heard that, Caleb. You growing boys! If you change your mind about dinner, you can help yourself. It's on the stove." She led me into the dining room.

"Hey, Caleb." Austin's mouth was full of spaghetti. His mom and Hillary simultaneously shook their heads in disgust. He shoved in another forkful without even noticing.

My attention turned toward the sound of the bubbling sauce in the attached kitchen. As if reading my mind, Austin's mom grabbed a plate from the cupboard and plopped a pile of steaming noodles on it.

"Go ahead. Sit. You have to try my spaghetti." She ladled the thick red sauce over the pasta.

"It's the best," Austin said while chewing his mouthful. His mom smiled at him. Hillary rolled her eyes.

"So, you're Caleb. The prankster, right?" said Austin's father. He was a tall, thin man with graying hair and a wide chin.

"I . . . uh . . .I shouldn't have done that," I stammered.

"Oh, whatever, Caleb. Everyone could use a good scare now and then. Right, Austin?"

Austin was focused on his plate again, but he gave a subconscious nod as he bit into his thick slice of sourdough bread. Hillary smiled at me.

"So, you kids are going back to the museum tonight? Are you sure that's a good idea?" Austin's dad asked.

"I already told you like a hundred times, Dad," Austin said. "Lilly lost her earring and we need to go back in and find it."

"I know. I know. I guess I just don't like you kids wandering around in there." He raised an eyebrow at Austin.

Austin finished chewing and swallowed. "We'll be fine, Dad."

"Matthew Bradford wasn't fine."

Austin's Mom placed a plate piled high with spaghetti and a slice of bread in front of me.

"Eat up, Caleb. You'll like it."

Austin glanced over at my plate and back to his almost empty one. For a minute, I was sure he was going to attempt a switch-up.

"If we find out what happened to him, maybe people would start coming again. Maybe we could reopen it." Austin shoveled another fork-load into his mouth.

"Wait, you guys own the museum?" I asked.

"Yeah. Matt Bradford's family owned it before we did. His great-grandfather built the museum. It used to be a real big deal. Matt's dad closed it down after he took ownership. He was planning a big renovation. That's when Matt went crazy. After they found his son dead, Mr. Bradford wanted nothing to do with the museum. He just gave my dad the property and his family moved away." Austin's dad leaned back in his chair.

"So, he just gave you the museum?" That sounded crazy, but no crazier than most of what I'd seen here in Ambler.

Austin's dad scratched at his rather large nose. "Yeah. He said we'd be able to do something with it, but

69

I don't have the money to invest in getting it back up and running. Even if I did, I don't know if people would go into the museum after what happened to Matthew."

"Really, Nick? You talk about *that* just before these kids go back there?" Austin's mom shook her head. "That story about how poor Matthew died is probably one hundred percent nonsense, kids. No one really knows what happened."

"I know what happened," Austin's dad persisted. "I talked to Mr. Bradford. He told me everything. Why would he have lied to me?"

"Oh, who knows? Just don't get the kids all worried before they go over there. Look, Caleb hasn't even touched his dinner."

The food had completely slipped my mind. Austin's mom watched me until I took a bite.

"That is really good," I said.

"Oh, I'm glad you like it. Now, where's Lilly?"

"I'm sure she's on her way," Austin said.

What if she wasn't? What if she was already at the museum? What if she already had the watch? Darkness filled my heart as the thought crossed my mind, like the sun being overshadowed by a storm cloud.

The doorbell rang and Austin's mom jumped up to answer it. I tapped my fork on the plate.

"Oh, hello, Lilly. It's good to see you again."

"Hi, Mrs. Harris."

I arched my neck so I could see the doorway. It was her, bundled up in a beige wool overcoat. She was unraveling a red scarf from around her neck. The darkness I felt disappeared with one look at her.

"Psst! Don't stare. Remember what I told you?" Hillary whispered. I shook it off and nodded. Lilly walked into the dining room. I took a massive bite of sourdough bread as she sat across from me at the table.

"Would you like some spaghetti, Lilly?" asked Austin's mom.

"It smells wonderful. May I have a little?"

"Of course you can. What fantastic manners. Do you hear that, Austin? That's what good manners sound like. He hasn't heard those since Maggie left for college, have you Austin?"

"Everything I know about good manners, I learned from you, Ma." Austin smirked.

"Not true. You got your good looks from me and your manners from your father. Do you see what you've taught him, Nick?"

Austin's dad didn't answer with words. Instead, he let fly a powerful burp that rattled the silverware on the table. Austin's mom stopped breathing.

"I'm sorry, honey. Were you saying something?" Mr. Harris smiled wide. Austin's mom grabbed a roll of paper towels off the counter and bonked him over the head with it.

"That's it, Mr. Disgusting! It seems we need to have another one of our private chats about how to behave when there's company!"

Austin's dad cowered as she hit him again. "Oh, come on. It was a joke."

"Now!"

Mr. Harris stood up slowly. He turned back toward us and beamed a wide grin. Austin chuckled as his dad quickly changed his expression back to sincere remorse and followed her out of the room.

"Man, I thought they'd never leave. So embarrassing." Austin grabbed the untouched piece of bread from his mom's plate and bit in.

"So, I'm still confused." I put my fork down. "If you own the museum, then why don't you just go in whenever you want? Why did you need us to come with you?"

"Oh. That. Well, after what happened to Matt, my parents don't like me and Hillary going in there alone. Mom's always saying she doesn't think his death had anything to do with the museum. She says that all the time. I don't think she believes it, though. I think she's scared the same thing will happen to us."

"So why do you want to go back in there?" I popped the last bite of sourdough into my mouth.

"Curiosity mostly. I felt something in there. I'm not saying this to try and scare you. I really felt something. There's a dark presence in that museum, especially around that chest you found. I don't know what it is, but I'm gonna find out." Austin wiped buttery crumbs from his lips.

"Oh, right." I loaded my fork up with spaghetti. "The special powers thing. You see dead people, right?"

"I don't see them, Caleb. I just feel them. I know when they're near."

"And how do you know?" I asked.

"I get quiet. I listen and I feel. Most of the time I don't feel anything. Sometimes I feel happy. Other times I feel something dark."

I shook my head. Why would anyone believe him? "So, your special powers not only help you feel if ghosts are around, but they also help you tell if it is a good guy ghost or a bad guy ghost?"

"Why're you making fun of Austin, Caleb? We're not making fun of your special super-jerk powers," Lilly said.

"Ohhhhh. Burnnnnn!" Austin slapped Lilly a high five.

"I believe Austin," Hillary said. "I've been with him when he's experiencing a presence. I usually feel it, too. Just a little bit, but I do feel it."

I shook my head. These people were a couple sandwiches short of a picnic.

"Okay, so we're going back in to get Lilly's earring, but I'm also looking for the source of that negative energy I felt in the museum. I need you guys to be on the same page with me. If I tell you not to touch something or not to go into a certain room, you need to do what I say. Deal?"

"Deal," said Lilly and Hillary.

"I don't know. I don't believe in all of this ghost crap, but even if I did, why would I be afraid of ghosts? They're supposed to be see-through, right? And they can't even touch you because their hands would go right through you. Am I right? Why would you ever be afraid of something that can't hurt you?"

Austin gave me a grave look. "Because they *can* hurt you, Caleb. They can hurt you in more ways than you'd ever know."

We all stared at him for a moment. He was pretty convincing. He even had me going for a second or two.

"Come on." Austin stood up from the table and stretched his long arms over his head. "I've got some things to show you. They might change your mind about ghosts."

We followed him through the living room. Lilly walked to my left. I leaned over.

"Are you afraid?" I whispered.

"A little. How about you?"

"Of course not."

"Everyone's afraid of ghosts."

"Not me."

"Why not?"

"Because ghosts don't exist. They're not real."

"I hope you're right." Lilly tucked her bottom lip under her teeth as we followed Austin and Hillary into Austin's room.

There wasn't much space. I sat on the floor next to Lilly as Austin turned on his computer. Hillary sat on a nightstand that was next to his bed. His whole room smelled like moldy bread and sweaty tennis shoes. I looked over into the corner by his closet and saw both; an old sandwich sitting half-eaten on a shelf over a stack of dirty shoes representing at least five different sports. Gross.

Austin sat down in his desk chair and swiveled toward us, a book in his hands. His computer hummed as it slowly came to life.

Austin opened the cover of the book. It was leather-bound, with thick pages and no title on the front. The cover was hardened and cracked with age. This was no novel or dictionary.

"What's that?" Lilly asked.

"This is a journal," Austin said. "It's the journal of Henry Harris, my Great-Great-Grandfather."

"Wait. *That* Henry Harris?" Lilly asked.

"Yeah."

Austin's shoulders slumped, but he continued to search the pages. My forehead wrinkled. I guessed everyone in Ambler knew who Henry Harris was, but I sure didn't.

"Henry Harris was the engineer of the train that crashed in 1856." Hillary to the rescue. She nodded at me as if testing my understanding of her explanation.

"You're related to the guy who crashed the train?"

Hillary froze mid-nod and scowled at me. Austin stopped flipping.

"Oh, sorry, guys. I. . . ."

"It's okay. You didn't know." Austin faked a smile at me. This was a real sore topic for them.

"Austin! You forgot to take the garbage out!" Austin's mom shouted from the kitchen.

"Oh crap," Austin muttered. He didn't move.

"Austin! Don't make me come in there! I have your baby album and I know your friends would love to see it!"

Austin jumped out of his chair. "Be right back."

Lilly grabbed the journal from Austin's desk. "I wonder what he wrote before that day."

"Before he... died?" I craned my neck to see the pages.

"Be careful with that," Hillary said.

Lilly skipped through the blank pages near the end to the first page covered in loopy handwriting.

"What're you doing?" Austin said. He stood in the doorway, munching on a piece of leftover sourdough bread.

"Just looking to see the last thing he wrote."

"Yeah. It's kinda creepy." Austin sat back down. "Read it out loud, Lilly."

"Let's see. Okay." Lilly focused to decipher the handwriting on the page. "When did that Great Train wreck happen again?"

"It was on July 17th, 1856," Austin said.

"Well, the last entry is from July 16th." Lilly glanced up at everyone to see if she should read it. Austin nodded.

"Okay. Here goes." She cleared her throat.

"I was up early this morning. I ran the Shakamaxon all day. After the third short route, I finished up around 5:15 P.M. After a lovely meal with my wife and son, I walked down to the train station to collect my paycheck. The girl at the counter said Mr.

*Blackwell wanted to talk to me. I have never
been comfortable around that man."*

"So Mr. Blackwell was his boss?" I asked.

"Yeah," Austin said. "Keep reading."

Lilly started again.

*"Blackwell told me I was doing a great job. I
was surprised to hear the words come out of his
mouth. As I said, he doesn't give compliments
easily. A very cold man. Then, he handed me
a box and told me it was a gift. He said it
was for all of my hard work and for taking
such good care of the passengers. I opened it."*

She stopped reading. Her mouth dropped open.

"What is it, Lilly?" I asked. I looked over her
shoulder to what old Mr. Harris had written. Lilly's index
finger hovered over a short sentence.

It was a watch.

I felt the color drain out of my face.

"Well, keep reading," Hillary demanded.

Lilly's expression gave it all away. She wanted it.
When had she seen it? Had she dreamed about it too?

Lilly took a deep breath and continued.

*"The watch was beautiful, gold with a pocket
chain. It had a picture of a train on the case
and everything. I have to admit I felt bad*

about how I usually talk about Mr. Black-
well. Maybe he's not such a bad fellow after
all."

"I thanked Mr. Blackwell and walked home.
It sure was a pretty night. I have an early
morning, so I'm off to bed. One last thing to
do: kiss my wife goodnight."

We sat in silence, pondering on the final written words of a man who died the next day.

Finally, Hillary broke the silence. "So, Austin has a theory."

I sat up straight, hands shaking. They all knew about the watch.

I had to get it before they did.

"It might sound like I'm just defending my great-great-grandpa," Austin said, his head bowed. "But Blackwell sounds like a strange man. Something was off about him."

Hillary butted in. "And he gave our great-great-grandpa the watch."

"So what?" I wanted the subject changed immediately.

"Don't you remember why the train wreck happened?" Hillary asked.

"Time," Austin said. "The Shakamaxon left the

station very late. What if it was all caused because the watch Blackwell gave him was set slow?"

"I thought you were going to tell us a ghost story." I folded my arms. I had to shift everyone's attention from the watch. Especially Lilly's. She stared at those words on the page, her eyes tracing them over and over.

It was a watch.

"The watch is connected." Austin spun around in his chair to face his computer. "My theory comes from some information I found on this one website."

"It's the best place to go when you want to learn more about the realm of the paranormal." Hillary smiled proudly, obviously brainwashed by her older brother.

Austin typed some words into the search engine on his computer. I could read them over his shoulder:

DeadandLiving.com

CHAPTER 9

The lettering on the website's front page was jagged and made of tiny lines, like a mass of spider webs. The man who appeared next to the title looked nothing short of completely insane. His name appeared beneath the picture: Ed Creedy.

"Is this a joke?" I asked. Austin gave me an empty look, like his eyes didn't connect to his brain.

I pointed back to the image of the man. "Ed Creedy? Who is this guy?"

"Ed Creedy is an expert. He knows what he's talking about, Caleb." Austin's face went red. Defensive. "He's seen so many ghosts and he writes about all of them. He's gifted."

"Gifted?" I snorted. "Oh, like you?"

"No. I only wish I was as gifted as Creedy. He sees everything. He wants to know more, so he goes after it.

He looks for ghosts. He wants to understand them."

I rubbed my forehead. "This is ridiculous."

"No, it's not. I read an article a few weeks ago about ghosts that possess objects. Let's see if I can find it." Austin scrolled through the list of article headlines on the website. "See, objects involved in tragedies sometimes become a trap for the souls involved."

Hillary stood up and stared over Austin's shoulder. "Austin thinks the watch survived the accident. He thinks it's somewhere in the museum and that it's possessed."

I jolted upright.

"That's quite the assumption," Lilly said. "How would a watch survive a train crash that killed almost everyone aboard?"

I nodded. Then it dawned on me. She was just as defensive of the watch as I was. She definitely knew about it.

Austin kept scrolling through article titles. "I'm not sure. All I know is what I felt. What I heard."

"And what did you feel and hear?" I asked.

Austin swiveled to look at us, his eyes wide. "I felt I was in a crowd. I heard their voices. They were... they were terrified."

Hillary leaned against her brother's shoulder. "Austin wants to find the watch or whatever it is and destroy it. He thinks people stopped coming to the museum because something in the place has a bad vibe. Maybe that watch."

Destroy the watch? Yeah. Not happening.

"Maybe people didn't want to come because it was totally boring. That's a way more logical explanation," I said. Austin ignored me and skimmed over article after article. I was less and less convinced with each title that rolled by.

Why Ghosts dislike Fast Food.

Is your Cat Possessed?

Nine Household Chores Ghosts will do for You.

and, of course; *Shoe Obsessed Spirits: The Footwear of the Dead.*

I shook my head.

"Here it is. *Object Possession: Haunted Hiding Places.*" Austin took a deep breath and started reading.

> "A woman I met in Minnesota said that her grandfather's favorite chair would start rocking any time someone started a fire in the fireplace. A man in Maryland claimed that his deceased mother-in-law still resides in the backseat of his car where her spirit will sometimes call out loud critiques of his driving. Object possession is a reality in the realm of the dead. If you know of a possessed object, I would advise you, my curious reader, to beware. You may just be dealing with a

spirit that has separation anxiety, or you may
be dealing with something far more sinister."

"Can we just go get my earring?" Lilly was getting
impatient. But I knew it wasn't just the earring she
wanted.

"No. You guys gotta know what you're up against
before we go back into the museum. I'm gonna keep
reading. Pay attention!"

"Fine." Lilly crossed her arms over her chest.

Austin turned back to the screen.

"Case in point, the Hoosac Mountain in Mas-
sachusetts. When I entered the tunnel, I felt
a dark essence emanating from a section of
the track. A railroad spike especially. I knelt
down. The closer I came to it, the more my
hands began to tremble.A raspy voice whispered to me from the ground, 'Tell me your
name and hold tight to the tracks. All will be
revealed.'

I knew better than to do what it said. The
statement was far more a threat than an in-
vitation.

Another voice cried out to me.

'Don't listen to him. He's a murderer.'

'Who are you?' I asked.

Then I heard screaming."

"That Creedy dude must've looked super sane

kneeling down talking to the railroad track," I interrupted.

Hillary gave me a dirty look. Austin shook his head
and plowed along.

> "I made out a name, Billy Nash, before they
> all fell silent. A chill came off the tracks. No
> matter how I cajoled afterward, I couldn't
> get any more responses from the spirits con-
> tained within."

Austin nodded his head at me. "See that? Spirits.
Trapped inside the spike."

Like his stupid ghost story proved anything.

"Can't we just get going?" I motioned to the door
with my thumb.

Austin ignored me and continued.

> "The Hoosac Tunnel has a bloody history.
> Two hundred miners lost their lives while the
> tunnel was being bored through the mountain
> rock. In March of 1865, the foreman, Ringo
> Kelly, set off the blast while two other men
> were still in the tunnel. The men were killed
> in the explosion and Kelly disappeared. One
> year later, Kelly's corpse was found in the
> exact same spot where his coworkers died.
> He had been strangled to death. The names
> of the two men that had died in the explosion
> the year previous were Ned Brinkman and
> Billy Nash."

He paused for dramatic effect, then cleared his throat.

> "Since the beginning, people who have lived lives of evil have tried to find ways to avoid moving on into the next life for fear of judgment of one type or another. They will do anything to remain bound to the physical realm, even bind their spirits into tiny objects, tucked away where no one will find them. In the case of Ringo Kelly, I have determined from my observations that he had planned the deaths of his fellow workers and his own."

"That's a dumb story." I tried to play it off. The truth was, Austin had started to get to me. My hands were shaking.

Austin only paused for a second before he started reading again.

> "And so, brave reader, I bid you beware of ghosts that inhabit objects. They may be a more menacing presence than you could have ever imagined. The one I met in Massachusetts was just as possessive of the souls he had imprisoned as he was of the item they inhabited. Had I followed his request, I may have become his prisoner as well.
>
> Happy Hauntings!
>
> *-Ed Creedy*"

I was about to make a wisecrack, but Austin and Hillary both stared me down with that *don't-you-dare* look. I smirked as quietly as I could.

Lilly bit her lower lip. "So, ghosts in a watch?"

"Yeah." Austin clapped his laptop shut. "Ghosts in a watch."

"Do... do you think there's a connection between the watch and what happened to Matt Bradford?" Lilly's eyes were different. The fire from before had been replaced by cold fear.

Austin shrugged. "Not sure. Could be. From what Creedy said, touching the possessed item could have a bad effect."

I stood up. "So are we gonna do this or what?"

"I'm ready." Hillary jumped up and ran for the door.

"Wait up, Hill. If you don't wear a jacket Mom will kill me." Austin chased her out the door. Those two transitioned between ghost stories and hyperactivity pretty easily.

Lilly sat still, her face more pale than usual.

"You okay?" I asked.

"Yeah." She took a deep breath.

"Are you ready to go find your earring?"

"I guess so." Her eyes drifted to the old book in her hands and then back to me.

"Caleb, what are you afraid of?" Her eyes were so

sincere. For a minute I couldn't even speak.

"Not a train museum," I answered, trying to hide the quake in my voice. "What about you? What're you afraid of?"

She closed her eyes. Her lips tightened. "A lot of things."

When she looked at me again, her eyes were full of tears. "What about you?"

I waited, my hand on the doorframe. I was afraid. So afraid. But I couldn't tell her. She would never understand.

"One thing," I said. "Just one."

CHAPTER 10

Austin's apartment complex wasn't far from the museum, so we walked. Icy wind gusts seeped through my coat and right into my bones. But that wasn't the only reason I was quaking. A feeling of terror rose up inside of me. There was also regret. In my mind, I could see my mom's face, tears streaming down her cheeks because of what I'd said.

But didn't she deserve it? Why was she so focused on forcing me to go see him?

And when I came back with the watch, would I even be scared anymore? I saw it in my mind, the gold shining warmly, filling my body. No need for fear. No need for regret. Only confidence and power.

Lilly looked over her shoulder at me, her face both cautious and conniving. What was going on in her head? Austin and Hillary walked in the lead, oblivious to anything going on behind them.

A commuter train blasted by on the track. Its headlight blazed a path through the dark night. I could almost make out the faces of the passengers as it flew past, fleshy blurs against lit windows, their heads bowed in boredom or sleep. The whistle bellowed and the train was gone, leaving only a rattle on the tracks behind.

The museum stood before us, its weather-beaten exterior dark and rotting. Street lights illuminated the jagged grain of the ancient wood. Just next door was the restaurant that had once been the actual train station. What had it looked like on the day of the accident? How many tears fell on that floor when the train never returned the passengers to their families?

Austin knelt down beside the lock and fit the key into the keyhole. It clacked open in his hands. He pulled the door open and clicked on his flashlight.

"Stay close to me," Austin said. There was no need to tell Hillary. She'd been very brave before we left the house, but now she was pressed so close to him that I could barely see her behind his lanky silhouette.

The ticking filled my ears. It was here, calling to me. I was only footsteps away from the watch.

The question was how to get the Ghost Whisperer and his sister away from me so I could get it without anyone knowing.

Austin led us through the reception area, past the huge steam engine, and into the hallway. The ticking stopped.

Creeeaaaak.

I froze, my heartbeat pounding. Darkness in the cracks and corners of the room writhed like dancing demons.

Creeeeeaaak. The sinewy shadows spread out and wove together like oily spider webs. They spiraled into a wheel and then an armrest, winding together to form a head and dead white eyes.

Creeeeeaaak. The squeak of rubber against metal. Cold sweat on my forehead. His wheelchair rolled toward me. His face hung limp. I backed away.

"Lilly!" Hillary cried out.

I turned from the blank stare of my father. Lilly convulsed on the floor. I ran and dropped to my knees beside her. The shadows wrapped around her, coiled around her mouth and nose. As I moved closer, she thrashed uncontrollably. The blackness was completely covering her, wrapping her tight like a mummy.

I stared back over my shoulder. My father closed in on us, staring vacantly. I didn't know what to do.

I pinned her shoulders down to the ground. The moment that my hands connected with her, the shadows moved away. They slipped back into the corners and under cobweb covered furniture.

My father was gone. I couldn't believe what I'd just seen. Lilly lay still.

Austin and Hillary ran to her. I shook her lightly.

"Lilly? Lilly? What happened? Are you okay?" Her eyes opened slowly. She sucked in a breath.

"Oh. I . . . I thought I was dreaming. I thought I was . . . ."

"What happened?" Hillary panted. Austin's flashlight beam shone directly on Lilly's face. She shielded her eyes.

"I'm fine. I don't know what happened. Could you stop pointing that thing in my eyes?"

"Sorry. Just making sure you're okay. Did you trip or something?" Austin asked.

"Yeah. I tripped. That's all." Lilly's voice was high pitched and sweat dripped from her forehead.

I spun around, but all I saw were shadows in a corner. No wheelchair. No writhing shadow worms.

"Caleb?" Austin said.

"I'm fine, too," I lied.

"Okay." His forehead creased. "I'm getting some weird vibes. Are you guys feeling anything?"

I looked at Lilly, lying on the ground, her face pale. I helped her to her feet.

"I'm fine," she repeated. "I'll be more careful."

Austin shook his head. "Let's go." He walked further down the hallway. Hillary glanced over her shoulder, her eyes wide, knees wobbling. Then she followed him.

We continued into the darkness. The shadows shifted again but this time I thought about the watch. I could see the old man holding it out to me. The second I thought of it, the shadows fell still. Soon, I would hold it in my hand, and its golden glow would surge through me.

No more fear.

We came to the room where I'd played my prank, the room where Matthew Bradford had died. Austin put his arm out to stop us as we entered.

"There is definitely something in here. I can feel it. Can anyone else feel it?"

"I think I sort of feel it," Hillary said.

Lilly scanned the room. "I don't feel anything."

"Yeah, me neither."

I was lying again. There was something dark in there. Every thump of my heart told me so. But it couldn't be the watch. The watch was my way out of being afraid. It was confidence in a physical form.

I was pretty sure Lilly was lying too. A shiver trembled down her body.

"I'm sure I feel something." Austin blared his

flashlight around the room. "I think it may be coming from that chest you found last night, Caleb."

"There wasn't anything in there. Just my fake ghost."

"I think Caleb's right. There isn't anything in there." Lilly faced away from the chest, stiff as a rail. Austin raised a bushy eyebrow.

"You guys are acting weird."

"No, we're not," Lilly said.

"Yeah, you're the one who's acting weird." I forced my gaze away from the chest. Austin glared at me.

"Isn't this where you lost your earring, Lilly?" I asked, ignoring Austin. "Let's look for it. Austin, why don't you guys head on down to the next room and look around? If there's some possessed object, we'll find it faster if we split up."

I stared him down, hoping he believed me. It became very obvious he didn't.

"No, really. What's going on?" Austin asked. I tried to think fast. I needed to find some way to get them out of the room.

"Austin?" Hillary tugged on her big brother's sleeve. "Can we please go into the other room? I'm getting scared."

"Come on, Hill!" Austin turned to her. "You said you weren't gonna get like this if I let you come along."

"I can't help it. What Dad said. About Matthew dying here." A teardrop slid down her cheek.

Austin huffed out a breath. "Fine! But we'll be back in a minute or two. I know you two don't believe me, but I'm getting a really weird vibe from that chest over there. A really dark vibe. Don't touch it."

"Oh, okay. We'll just be here looking for the earring." I pointed to the dingy floor. "We won't touch the chest."

Austin nodded.

"I hope you find your earring, Lilly. Come on, Hillary."

Austin and Hillary walked off as I pulled a flashlight from my backpack and clicked it on. Lilly stared at the chest.

"Where do you think your earring landed? Probably somewhere over there?" I suggested, pointing to an area on the other side of the room.

"Yeah, you should go look for it." She edged toward the chest, cautious at first, watching me from over her shoulder.

The fear in my heart burned black. I lunged toward the chest. Lilly did the same. As I flew past her, she dove for my legs. I tumbled to the dusty floor. Lilly was in front of me, reaching out for the old wooden box. I grabbed for her arm, catching her thin wrist in my grasp.

96

I would slam her arm against the ground, maybe break it. Then she could never get the watch. It would be mine.

As my fingers connected with her flesh, my mind cleared. I'd planned to *break* Lilly's arm? Over a *watch*? What in the world was wrong with me? I let go of her wrist. She reached out and slashed at my face with her fingernails. I fell back in pain. Lilly jumped up, triumphantly.

I lay on the cold floor, clutching my bleeding face. The gashes stung my cheek, but not as much as the fact that she'd done it. She stopped dead in her tracks, her eyes wide. Austin ran into the room with Hillary close behind.

"What happened?" he demanded. Tears dripped down Lilly's cheeks.

"I'm so sorry, Caleb. I'm so sorry. I don't know what got into me."

I sat up slowly. I had just as much to be sorry for as she did. More actually. We were ready to hurt each other, and badly, just for some old pocket watch.

"Tell me what's going on. No lies this time," Austin said. His voice boomed through the museum and echoed off the walls. Lilly wiped her eyes and tried to look at me.

"You didn't lose your earring, did you, Lilly?" Austin asked.

"No."

"Why did you want Caleb to come?"

"I thought he might distract you or something."

"Why did you want Caleb to distract me, Lilly?"

"I don't know. Ever since I saw it, I've needed it. I don't know why."

"What are you talking about?"

I stood and wiped the blood off of my cheek.

"I can tell you," I said. "I've been going through the same thing."

Austin, Hillary, and Lilly stared at me like I was from another planet.

"It's the . . . ."

As the words formed on my lips, I saw it in my mind. Golden. Glorious. The old man held it out to me, just within my grasp. My feet stepped toward the chest. Almost automatically.

"Caleb, no," Lilly shouted. She ran at me.

"Yes, Caleb," a raspy voice whispered in my ear. "Take it. Take it fast. He's coming."

The squeal of rubber on metal tore into my ear drums. The wheelchair formed from the corner shadows in seconds. My father rolled toward me, his body sagging and limp, the chair rolling itself forward.

No time to be afraid. Freedom from fear was only a few feet away.

I turned and ran toward the chest. Pressure wrapped around my leg and I fell again, slapping the floor with my open palms.

"Stop, Caleb! It's not safe!"

"Don't get in my way again, Lilly."

"Both of you! Stop!" Austin shouted.

Hillary screamed.

"It's mine!" Lilly shrieked and lunged toward the chest. I grabbed her around the waist and tossed her to the floor. She slid across and bumped against the wall. The shadows in the corner of the room reached for her and pulled her down beneath them. She struggled against them as they rippled over her. She grasped her throat in agony, fighting for breath. I turned to face my father.

"You'll never be afraid again, Caleb," the voice whispered in my ear.

The wheelchair came closer.

Behind me, Austin's feet pounded hard against the wooden floor.

I flipped the lid of the chest open.

"No!" Lilly screamed. She pulled herself free from the shadows and grabbed for me.

I had the watch. It was in my hand. Lilly pushed me with all of her strength. I fell to the ground with an echoing thud. The watch slid from my hand. Lilly reached for it.

"Open me," the voice whispered. "Open me, and come home."

Austin pulled on my shoulder, wrenching me away from the watch. I kicked him in the face and crawled forward.

The watch was within reach. I stretched to grab it. Austin's hand coiled around my ankle.

I felt the smooth cover. I positioned it in my hand, the knob on the top nestled snugly under my thumb. Lilly slammed into me again. This time I didn't let go. I pressed down on the button. Lilly reached out for the watch.

The watch flicked open. Lilly was touching it. I was touching it.

"No!" Austin shouted.

It's impossible to describe what happened next. The closest comparison I could make was a powerful vacuum cleaner sucking out my insides as I desperately tried to hang on to them. Lilly screamed beside me. Her eyes shook violently and her body went limp. She dropped to the floor.

What had I done?

I couldn't hold on any longer. The watch face grew larger, the hands as big as bridges. My lifeless body lay behind me as I was sucked into the watch.

CHAPTER 11

Maybe I was closing my eyes, although I don't know how that would've been possible since I no longer had eyes or eyelids. I mean, I saw my body drop.

I was dead. I was literally dead.

But I did open my eyes. Somehow. I did see.

It was very dark. My senses were dulled, but I still felt the bite of cold. An orange light shone brightly on the metal floor beneath me. I lay there, just trying to feel.

There was silence in my temples where I usually felt the drumbeat of my pulse, and stillness in my chest where my lungs should have been pumping. Things I never had to think about doing were now impossibly gone. I panicked a little, tried to take deep breaths, but, again, no lungs.

My pain was also gone. I remembered the sting of Lilly's nails on my cheek, but I couldn't feel it. There was a different kind of pain, though. Guilt. Fear. I was freaking out, and that feeling *felt* like it was oozing out of my body.

And it was.

Blobs of blackness dripped out of my pores. I sat up and tried to wipe it off. The more terrified I became, the more the black stuff leaked out. I had to calm down. I tried to think about something else. Something besides the fact I was dead.

Where was I? Was any of this real or was I more in need of a psychologist than my mom or I ever knew? As I calmed down, the black stuff stopped flowing. The puddle that had formed at my feet began to quiver. It scuttled away like a fat spider.

I pushed myself up from the ground. It was easier than it should've been, like gravity had been reduced by at least thirty times.

The ground below me was silver and etched with a wavy pattern that looped away into the distance. Even in the dark, I could see fine. Maybe it was because the eyes of the dead don't need light to see. Maybe it was because of the white-orange light surrounding me.

Wait.

The light was coming *from* me. From my chest. A

glowing orb where my heart should've been.

"What in the. . . ." I jumped at the sound of my own voice in that silent place. Words had actually come out of my mouth. This being dead thing wasn't all that different than being alive.

But was I dead?

The floor jolted, throwing me forward. I slid across metal on my stomach, clawing at the slick ground. I rolled to my right to stop the forward momentum. My body skidded to a stop, my head hanging over a long, dark fall.

I stared over the edge of a massive gear. The teeth lining it were as big as the battlements on a castle. The drop below was about thirty feet. I'd barely stopped myself from plunging over the side to my death.

But I couldn't die. Could I?

I pushed myself away from the ledge and crawled back toward the middle of the disk.

Another orange light illuminated the far side of the gear. I strained my eyes to see what it was coming from.

"C-C- Caleb?"

Lilly.

I ran to her.

"Are you okay?" I knelt beside her. She was covered in black slime.

"Caleb?" she asked again through soft sobs.

103

"Yeah. It's me."

"Where are we?"

"I don't know."

"Are we . . . dead?"

"I think so." I didn't know what else to say. Lilly sobbed even harder. I put my hand on her back as she cried. The warmth of her skin was gone. She was as cold as the stale air around me.

"How did this happen?"

"I'm not sure." I shook my head. Austin must've been right all along. "It was that watch. It must've been some sort of a trap. We touched it and it killed us."

"But where are we?"

Just as she finished her question, the ground jolted again. We steadied ourselves.

"We're dead," Lilly sobbed. "We're dead!"

"We're in the watch, Lilly. Somehow, we're inside of it."

"I want to go home." Her tears were streams of blackness.

"You need to calm down, Lilly."

She turned on me, eyes blazing. "Don't tell me to calm down, Caleb! This is your fault. We're dead because of you!"

Part of me knew she was right. Part of me wanted to yell right back at her. We came back for her earring, but that'd been a lie. This was her fault too.

But I knew she was more right than wrong. I'd been obsessed, ready to hurt her. She was trying to stop it all. She'd told Austin about the watch. I was the one who wouldn't let go.

Pools of blackness welled up around Lilly. They streaked across the silver floor, dripping off the edge of the gear. Blame could wait. For now, I had to get Lilly to stop making creepy, living puddles.

"Lilly. I'm sorry." I stood up. "But we're here, trapped in the watch now. If there's some way out, we're not going to find it by sitting here."

"This can't be real. I must be dreaming."

Dreaming? That actually made more sense than any other conclusion. Maybe in a minute or two, I'd wake up in my bed, with my mom, the Tin Man, Scarecrow, and the Cowardly Lion all around me. Smiling.

"You're not dreaming," came a voice from behind us. "But if you were, this'd be a nightmare."

I spun around. The gear jolted again and we almost fell. Some guy in brown slacks and a matching bow tie stood about three feet from us. He was wiry thin with brown hair and green eyes.

And he was transparent.

A ghost.

"My name's Will." He snapped his suspenders. Lilly

and I backed away.

"Who are you?" Lilly asked.

"Didn't I just tell you my name? Come on. I know you're scared, but we need to clear out of here."

"We're not going anywhere," I said.

Will stared at the light emanating from my chest. "Not one to trust a ghost you just met, huh?"

I took another step back. "No."

"Well, you'd think we'd have all sorts of time since we're dead, but it's kinda urgent I get you to Mr. Redmond. We'll have to build trust later. Can't let Darkwater get a hold of those Glows of yours."

"What're you talking about?" I stopped, my back against the brass column in the center of the gear.

Will palmed his forehead. "Ugh. This one's not so bright." He stepped closer, his eyes wide. "No time. Do you understand?" He pointed to Lilly, himself, and me. "We need to. . . ," he flattened one hand and walked his other hand across it on his fingers. ". . .go."

Lilly spoke up. "We're not stupid. We're just really confused."

Will turned toward the gear's edge. "Follow me. He'll be coming for you. We need to get you hidden."

"Who will be coming for us?" Lilly asked.

Will turned to us and shook his head. His eyes narrowed.

"Darkwater," he said.

I stepped between him and Lilly. "Who's that?"

"Pretty sure he's the devil." Will turned around. "Come on," he said, as he stepped off the edge of the gear.

"No!" I shouted. Lilly and I ran to the edge and peered down to the ground below. Will had landed, unharmed.

"He's a ghost. He's fine." Lilly stepped to the ledge and wiped black streaks from under her eyes. "We are too."

Will surveyed the area and then looked up and beckoned to us.

"Hurry up!"

The gear lurched and Lilly and I fell forward, barely keeping our balance.

"Should we trust him?" I asked.

"Do we have a choice?" Lilly stepped off.

I shook my head. This was insane.

But Lilly was right. What choice did we have?

"Geronimo," I whispered. And I jumped.

I fell slowly and softly and landed right next to Lilly.

"We made it." Her eyes were wide, but she smiled despite it all.

Will flapped his arms at us. "Come on! We need to

move." He took off running across the flat silver ground. We followed.

I could barely take in everything around me. The whole world was metal, shiny and shadowy. The ground was a stretch of silver, etchings running beneath our feet and off into the distance. Behind us, towers of brass gears rose above, like living skyscrapers. Their teeth flicked, creating a chain reaction of movement. A thick metal cylinder rose up from the ground in front of us. Mists of darkness wrapped around it, almost completely shrouding the bronze. A cold chill filled me as I looked at it.

"Keep your eyes off the dark tower," Will shouted.

"The what?" I asked. He didn't answer.

"Where are we going?" Lilly called ahead.

"To see Mr. Redmond," Will answered without looking back.

"Who's that?"

"He's our protector. He keeps us safe from Darkwater when he can."

"Do you know how we can get out of here?" I asked.

"If I did, do you think I'd still be here?"

Good point.

We ran on and on. I wasn't even winded. Then I remembered I wasn't breathing.

"How'd you two end up here?" Will turned his head

toward us but continued running.

"We touched a weird, old watch and now we're here." I widened my stride to try to match Will's pace. He was so fast.

"Ha! Just like someone else I know." He bolted ahead, even faster than before.

"There's more people in here?" Lilly asked.

"Yeah. Mostly a bunch of ankle-biters. A few older kids, like me, and then there's Mr. Redmond."

"How did you get here?" Lilly asked.

Will flinched. "There'll be time for stories later. For now, let's get you to safety."

Lilly and I followed him through the world of gears and metal. Everything had happened so fast. In the silence, my mind wandered. My nightmares. How I'd treated my mom. The fight with Lilly.

Guilt.

I could still feel it. It slopped to the ground behind me with every footfall.

We came across a row of rounded lumps rising from the metal ground. Polished and deep red. "What are these?" Lilly asked.

"These are the jewels of the watch." Will pointed at them as if he were our evil-watch tour-guide. "Rubies. They keep the gears on level two running smoothly with little to no friction."

"They're beautiful." Lilly stared at them, their red hazy light illuminating her face.

"When I was alive, I used to take apart watches as a hobby. Old broken ones my dad collected. Tried to fix 'em. Mostly just made 'em worse, though. I told everyone we were in a watch when we first got here. No one believed me. They all thought we were in hell."

"Are you sure we're not?" I asked.

"Nope. Not really. But if we are, then hell is inside a pocket watch made in London, England." He pointed to the words etched into the silver below our feet. Huge letters stretching off into the distance:

MADE IN LONDON, ENGLAND 1856

"Where are we going?" Lilly's voice shook.

"There're three levels in this watch. Right now we're on the highest, just below the face. Best hiding places are on level two, so that's where we're going."

We stopped in front of a sea of gears, spanning out below us, all the way to the curve of the wall. They moved together like gnashing teeth, gnawing at each other to rotate hands above.

"I'm not going down there." Lilly trembled, a few black streaks falling from her arms.

"Don't be afraid. Just jump," Will said. "Those gears can't touch you now. You're dead, you know?"

"This keeps getting worse and worse." More of

the black stuff slid down Lilly's cheeks. As it splattered to the ground, the drips flocked together and streaked away.

"Darkwater already knows you're here." Will stepped to the edge. "You have to trust me. We need to go now. Mr. Redmond will explain everything when we get there."

Will dropped off the edge and slipped between the teeth of the gears. Lilly watched him go, her lips tight. She closed her eyes and stood by the edge.

"Lilly–" I started. Before I could say anything else, she stepped off. She disappeared behind a clacking gear.

I jumped too.

We drifted toward the ground. I took in the sur-roundings in quiet awe. Level two was a living mass of gears. Some were spinning fast, while others remained still, waiting for the perfect moment to lurch forward. Metal pillars stuck through the centers of the gears, made of bronze and nickel. The main pillar dropped from the center of the watch, covered in the grey mist that I'd seen earlier. Will had called it the dark tower, and I could see why.

Just below the ceiling of level two, a face had formed on the shrouded pillar made from black ooze. Cruel eyes bled oily blackness, and the wide open mouth vomited a great waterfall of black water, which crashed down into a moat below. The dark tower dropped into the center of some kind of fortress. It looked like a castle that had been put in the microwave. The walls oozed and bubbled like hot tar. Four jet black towers stood in the corners, leaning limply inward, dripping with shadowy essence.

"What is that?" Lilly stood by Will, hunched over, her hands on her knees.

"Don't look at it." Will wagged his index finger at her.

"Is that Darkwater?" Lilly asked.

"That's where he lives."

I landed beside them. "What is he?"

"Whatever he wants to be." Will glanced all around us, scouting the area.

"Keep going and don't look at the tower." Will turned to run. "There are rules here. If you don't follow them, bad things happen. Mr. Redmond helps us, but he can't help if we don't follow the rules."

"What kind of rules?"

"Don't look at the tower." Will took off.

"Yeah, I got that one." I ran behind him, "Any more?"

"That's the only one you need to worry about right now. Just follow me. Come on!"

I was confused. I mean, if we were ghosts and we

didn't need to be afraid of jumping off cliffs or being ground up by rotating gears, then why was he so afraid of Darkwater?

We ran so fast. The fortress was to our left, and several towers of gears were directly in front of us. All I had to do was keep my face pointed straight ahead and everything would be fine.

I'm not sure what it was that made me do it. Curiosity? Fear? Maybe just downright defiance of authority?

I turned my head to the left and took a long stare at the fortress. It was a truly ugly thing, rippling with the dark essence, bulging and bubbling. I followed the contours of the walls up to the main tower and that hideous face.

The sculpted face on the main tower stared right back at me. My mouth dropped open.

It roared, gurgling on the ooze. Black water blasted from its mouth and surged toward us like it was being sprayed out of a fire hose.

Will turned to me. "You looked! I told you not to look!"

Waves of pure fear splashed out of the moat and rushed right toward us.

"Run!" Will yelled.

CHAPTER 12

The spray crashed to the ground only a few feet from us. Dark water speckled the air. We ran as fast as we could.

Why had I looked? What was wrong with me? It was my fault. All of this.

The mist wrapped around my leg and I dropped to the ground on my stomach. Lilly fell beside me. Will froze. The water curled in front of him and formed into a pile of greasy black snakes, slithering over the top of one another. They opened their fanged mouths, forked tongues flicking. He turned to run, but more formed behind him. He was surrounded.

Dark water covered Lilly almost completely. She thrashed her arms and her legs. Black tendrils reached into her mouth and nostrils. She screamed silently, muted by her liquid prison.

To my right, I saw him. My dad in his wheelchair. He stared at me, his lip hanging limp, like when I'd seen him last. He rolled toward me. A hollow thumping in my chest, the memory of my beating heart. My father rolled nearer.

Lilly kicked and swatted her arms uselessly. Will stood paralyzed with fear. Black sweat poured down his forehead as the snakes coiled themselves around his arms and legs.

My dad stared at me with those pale blue eyes. I trembled. An inky tear blotted my cheek.

Lilly went limp, the black water streaming out of her mouth and nose. Black ooze dripped from her pores.

My dad rolled closer. I tried to look away, but I couldn't.

I couldn't move.

His face trembled and then burst open, black gunk melting away until he was nothing more than a blob of melted wax.

The black water pulled away from us. I stood, my knees wobbling. Lilly sat up. Dark teardrops streamed off her face into the rushing wave of dark water. Will coughed and vomited ooze as the snakes dissolved back into water and receded toward the edges of the watch in serpentine ripples.

"I told you not to look," Will coughed.

My teeth were chattering so hard I couldn't reply.

Lilly coughed up little wisps of inky liquid.

"Are you alright?" I asked.

Before she could answer, Will did.

"He's not through with us." His voice was shaking harder than ever. "He's just getting himself ready for the hunt."

"What do you mean, Will? What's going on?"

"We've got to get to Mr. Redmond. Come on!" Will wiped the fear drops off his brow and splattered them to the floor.

"What is this place?" Lilly trembled on the ground, holding her knees to her chest.

"No one's really sure." Another new voice.

Will smiled wide. "Mr. Redmond. Thank goodness."

I spun around. There stood a little old man in a light blue suit, smiling at us. The old man from my dreams.

"You."

He stretched his hand out. "What's your name, son?"

I backed away from him. He had lured me here. This was his trap.

"What's the matter with you?" Will asked.

"H-He's the one that made me want the watch. He's the reason we're in here."

Mr. Redmond waved his hands in front of him, like

he was fanning my words away.

"No, no, no. You must be mistaken, boy. If I could leave this infernal place, I would. I would get all of us out of here. I'm working on it, but I haven't learned all the secrets just yet."

Lilly and I exchanged glances. Had he shown up in her dreams too?

"Mr. Redmond has helped us ever since he found us," Will said. "You can trust him. He's hidden us from Darkwater so many times I lost count years ago."

I shook my head. "If he's such a great guy, then why did he keep appearing to me with the watch, making me want it?"

"My goodness." Mr. Redmond stepped back, his hand to his chest. "It would seem Darkwater is using my image to lure young people in. I guess that would make sense."

"Why does that make sense?" It didn't make any sense to me. Mr. Redmond pursed his lips and answered.

"Have you seen what Darkwater looks like? Have you? If you have, then you'll know his features wouldn't exactly make one want to follow him into this place, now would it? Quite the opposite, really."

He did have a point. I hadn't seen Darkwater yet, but I'd seen enough of his work to know that if I did see him, I wouldn't have gone near the watch.

"Will, where have you been?" Mr. Redmond asked.

Will kicked at the ground. "I went looking for a way out."

"We talked about this, Will." Redmond crossed his arms behind his back. "It's not safe to wander about. The children need you."

"I know. I know. I thought I'd do a little exploring, that's all. Then, I saw two balls of light dropping from the sky." He pointed to the darkness above us. "I haven't seen anything that pretty since before we came here. I used to go stargazing with my pa. When I'd see a falling star, Pa would tell me to make a wish."

He scratched at his head. "It may sound stupid, but I made a wish today. When I saw these two falling through the dark, I wished we could get out of here. I wished we could escape. Then I found them."

I'd been so freaked out by everything, I hadn't even noticed that neither Will or Mr. Redmond had orange orbs in their chests. Only Lilly and me.

"If all it took was wishing," Redmond began, "we'd have been out of here years and years ago." Mr. Redmond surveyed the area. "We need to get back to the children. We'll need a good hiding place. Darkwater will be after their Glows for sure."

"Excuse me." Lilly still had good manners even though she was dead. "What are Glows?"

118

Redmond cleared his throat. "Ah, young lady. Your Glow is your connection to your physical body. While your body still lives, your Glow shines. When your body dies, your Glow will be extinguished."

Lilly's eyes went wide. "You mean. . . we're not really dead?"

"Exactly." Redmond smiled at her.

"Did you used to have a Glow?" I asked.

"Good question. No. My body was already dead when I arrived here." Redmond's smile faded. "I was alive. I went to bed. When I woke up, I was here. That's all I know. I have guessed that I was murdered in my sleep and trapped here."

"How long have you been here?" Lilly had softened toward him. I didn't blame her. It was a relief to have someone around who at least kinda knew what was happening to us. Someone we could trust.

"We've all been here for a long time." Redmond glanced at us again, his eyes darting back and forth. "We've had no visitors until recently. Another like you, falling from the sky. What a surprise to have someone new join us after all of these years, and one with that odd Glow in his chest. We soon learned Darkwater wanted the Glow. He wanted it more than anything."

My Glow looked a little paler than when I'd first arrived. I wondered if that meant anything.

"Darkwater came after the last kid who showed up here with a Glow," Will said. "First he sniffed it out, just like he did with you two a few minutes ago. After that, Darkwater hunted him for days. Mr. Redmond tried to keep him safe, but, in the end, Darkwater stole it from him."

"That cannot happen again." Mr. Redmond rubbed his chin. "Darkwater will come after your Glows. What he does with them is very . . . unfortunate."

"Why does he want them?" Lilly asked.

"I think he wants to live again." Redmond stepped closer, his arms out wide. "He took the body for himself and used it to do horrible things before the body rejected him." Redmond pointed to my chest. "The orange color means your heart is still beating and your lungs are still breathing, even though your spirit is in here. After a while, the body dies. A body can't live for long without the spirit."

"How long do we have?" I asked.

"I'm not really sure. No one had ever come here with a Glow before Matthew."

Lilly's head jerked up. "Matthew? Matthew Brad-ford?"

Mr. Redmond nodded. "Why yes. Do you know him?"

"Yes." Lilly nodded. "I did. Before he died."

"What are your names?" Mr. Redmond asked.

"I'm Lilly and this is Caleb." Lilly stood up and stepped closer to Redmond.

"Well, Lilly and Caleb, I can promise you I will do everything in my power to help you hold on to your Glows."

His words brought a soft warmth. A glimmer of hope in the dark.

"Thank you, Mr. Redmond." Lilly clasped her hands together.

Mr. Redmond smiled. "Of course, my dear. We may be closer to getting out of here than ever before. I've recently made new discoveries that may be the key to escaping this dreadful place. But, for now, come with me. We've got to get back to the children. I fear Darkwater has another atrocity up his sleeve."

"Let's go." Will pointed to the right.

Mr. Redmond put out an arm to bar us from moving any further. "I'm afraid we're too late."

The sky filled with black blobs, circling us like vultures.

"Not again." Will's lips trembled, spots of dark water forming on his brow.

"What's happening?" I demanded. Will didn't answer. He pointed to an area of ground a short way off, near the wall of level two. The black water had pooled

121

there. The liquid flowed together and formed into a straight metal beam. Another stream became a wooden plank.

Lilly wiped her blackened eyes on her arm, leaving an ashy smudge.

"The children," Will whispered. "Anna."

"What's happening?" I asked again. Will turned to me, black ooze spewing from his body.

"He's coming. Building strength for the hunt. It's too late." His eyes were vacant, too afraid to focus.

Mr. Redmond sighed. "I'm so sorry you have to be a part of this."

Drips of water sped off into the distance. The murky liquid spread fast, crawling over the landscape like a demon centipede. It stretched on for miles.

Tracks. Railroad tracks.

A massive blob of black water formed in a misty heap on the tracks. Grey drips stretched like putty, weaving together, forming iron bars jutting out toward the track and a tall smokestack above.

I knew what it was. I'd seen black and white pictures in my history classroom. It was the Shakamaxon, the train that had crashed in 1856.

And then I was on the train, standing in the car behind the engine. A man appeared in front of me. He wore an old black coat over blue and white striped overalls. His back was to me, his shoulders quaking uncontrollably.

"I'm sorry. I'm so sorry," he wailed. Black drips melted to the floor from his eyes. More people appeared, crowding the train car. Will was right next to us. Younger children were crying. Older ones stood as still as statues.

The steam train lurched forward on the tracks, the metal wheels screeching across the rails. The children cried out in terror. Some of them threw their bodies at the sides of the train car, trying to escape. Black ooze dripped from my face and hands. The smokestack belched vapors of darkness. Will wrapped his arms around two girls. One was small with curly blond hair. She was crying. The other was almost as tall as Will with long brown hair. She buried her head in Will's chest, trembling.

"No, please, no. Not again. Please!" wailed the conductor.

The blast of the train whistle drowned him out.

We were surrounded by liquid terror. My father's face bulged out of the side of the train car, staring at me with his vacant eyes. The fire in the belly of the boiler crackled and hissed. As the train picked up speed, the screams of the children were washed away in the rush of air.

I peered up the track through the chalky fog. The train shot over the track. Wind whipped through my hair. The children cried louder.

Further ahead, a blurry shape materialized. It sped toward us. The children screamed and pointed. Others wrenched their eyes shut and collapsed to the floor of the car.

It was a train. Another train.

It was headed right for us.

CHAPTER

There was only one passenger on the train in front of us. His body was a melting glob of oily blackness with constantly shifting features. His nose drizzled in and out of existence under pale white eyeballs. The darkness oozed over his gnashing white teeth in bubbling strands. He wore an old-fashioned suit. His neck extended unnaturally from his white shirt collar, arched and crooked, like it had been broken. He had no ears or hair, only dripping shadow.

His hands hung out of the cuffs of his shirt, fingers dripping like strands of candle wax. He reached up and pulled on the chain hanging down from the whistle. As it trilled through the darkness surrounding us, he smiled. The most horrid smile I'd ever seen. A smile that grew broader with every scream and wail of terror that came from the mouths of the terrified children.

DREAD WATCH - JARED AGARD

The last thing I saw before I clenched my eyes shut was the smile on that demonic face, the glee in those rotted eyes, and its dripping lips going slack as its jaw opened wide when its eyes locked onto the Glow in my chest.

The noise was too much. I felt the collision in my entire body. I was thrown toward the fire, its tendrils licking at my face as the boiler exploded. My body hurtled through the air as the sounds of screams, splintering wood, and twisting metal filled my ears.

And then crying, all around me, and the slurp of black teardrops joining the stream of ooze flowing back to the fortress.

I sat up. I was on the track in a pool of dark water. The wreckage of the trains disintegrated, leaving the weeping children scattered around the slowly dissolving track.

Lilly was on the ground comforting the young girl I'd seen beside Will. She was crying the hardest. Lilly wiped her tears and wrapped her arms around the little girl.

"Don't touch her." The brown-haired girl ran toward us, waving her hands.

"Anna, she doesn't know. She's like Matthew." Will wiped the black goop from his face.

"Who are they, Will?" Anna pointed at us. "Where

did they come from?"

"From outside. They still have their Glows. They still got a chance."

"And that's why Darkwater came for us. Because of them." Anna's brown hair whipped around her head as she turned toward us.

Black slime trickled from my pores. Globs of my own guilt slid down my arms.

I caused this. All the tears of these little children. All their cries of pain. Lilly's death. If I had just left the watch alone. If I had just . . . .

The little girl pulled away from Lilly. Her eyes went wide as she saw the orange light emanating from Lilly's chest.

A collective gasp went through the group of trembling children. I looked down at my own glowing orange chest.

There was still hope. As long as it was still glowing, we could get out of here. I would make it up to them. Lilly and these trapped kids. Somehow, I'd find a way out of this place.

That one bright thought stopped the flow of dark water from my body. The pools of black water evaporated into the air, leaving it thick and murky.

"Where did you find them?" Anna pointed to us like we were big bags of trash, wrinkling her nose in disgust.

"Level one."

"Are you kidding me? You know you're not supposed to go off on your own, Will. How many times do we need to tell you?"

Will rolled his eyes. "Yes, Mother. From now on I'll be a good boy."

Anna gnashed her teeth like she wanted to re-kill him for saving us.

Lilly leaned toward me. "Did you see that thing driving the other train?"

"Yeah." The memory sent a shiver down my spine.

"I think that was Darkwater."

"I think you're right." I spun around. "Where's Mr. Redmond?"

Will and Anna argued quietly as Lilly peered behind us. "Probably with the other children. Taking care of them after all. . . all that."

"I guess." I tucked my fist under my chin.

"You still don't trust Mr. Redmond, do you, Caleb?" Lilly raised an eyebrow. An accusation.

"Was it him in your dreams, too? The guy who showed up with the watch?"

She shook her head. "No. Well, yes. But it couldn't have really been him. It was Darkwater pretending, like he told us."

Something didn't add up. I couldn't put my finger on it. Or maybe I was having trust issues again.

"You're not going to be happy until he takes you, too." Anna turned away from Will, her anger fizzling into dark tears trailing down her cheeks.

Will stepped closer to her. "Aww, don't cry, Anna. He's not going to take me. I'm careful."

She laughed. "Careful? You risked everything to bring these two back. You should've thought about how this would affect everyone, Will. Darkwater will come for them."

Will shook his head. "Doesn't matter. We're going to help them."

"All I know is we need to protect the little ones." Anna wiped the remaining ooze off her pale yellow dress. "I'm not sure we can do that while protecting the newcomers."

The little girl stood up. "We have to help them. They still have a chance to get out. Maybe we can help them find a way."

"Don't take his side on this, Grace. We can't keep taking risks. If you or Will were taken, I don't know what I'd do." Her body trembled as she wrapped her arms around herself, streaks of grey streaming to the ground.

Will crossed his arms over his chest. "Fear can't keep us from acting. We've been hiding for too long. I'm not going to stop trying to find a way out."

Anna stared at the ground. "You sound just like Fredrick did before he was taken."

Gears shifted into place above me with an echoing clack.

"You should listen to Anna, Will." Mr. Redmond walked toward us, the children following behind him. "Sometimes bravery and foolishness are almost the same thing."

Lilly leaned closer. "See? There he is, with the children. Just like I said."

I watched Redmond closely, examining his every move. The man smiled back at me, his face crinkling with dimples.

Another boy walked up from behind Mr. Redmond, but he was dressed in a black t-shirt and blue jeans. "If Darkwater knows where we are, shouldn't we get moving? He'll start hunting them soon."

"Matthew?" Lilly gasped.

"Lilly?" He stared at her, "Oh no. This can't be happening."

"Do you know this guy, too?" Will asked, pointing at me.

"No. Just this one. She was just a little girl the last time I saw her. I was friends with her older sister."

"Matthew Bradford?" I guessed.

"Yeah," he said. "That's me."

My eyes went to his chest immediately. There was no glowing orange light.

"Matthew's right. Darkwater knows everything he needs to know. He's seen your Glows himself. No time for dilly-dallying. We need to get to the hiding place immediately." Redmond pointed to our right. "Follow me."

"Let's go," Will bellowed. The children got in line behind Will as Anna began counting them off like an elementary school teacher taking roll.

"Looks like we didn't lose anyone this time. Let's make sure we follow all the rules to keep it that way." Anna glared at Will.

"Yeah, yeah," Will muttered. "Let's go."

We took off running, following Will's lead. It was incredible how fast we could move, how lightly our footsteps hit the ground. Lilly was beside me, and Matthew was right next to her. Redmond, Will, and Anna led the charge, scanning the area as we went.

"So, did you open the watch in the railroad museum?" I asked.

Matthew turned his head toward me as we ran. "Is that how you guys came here, too?"

"Yeah. It was so strange." Lilly pumped her arms. "The watch became like an obsession or something. I wanted it all the time. I even dreamed about it."

"Yup. The same thing happened to me." Matthew wiped his face with his sleeve.

"It did?"

He nodded. "The last time I went into that museum, I was going to take that watch and nothing would stop me. The second I opened it, I was in here."

We ran faster. Redmond leaped from the ground to an impossibly high gear and cleared it with no problem. The others followed him. Will waited beside every child as they took their turn at jumping.

Could I do that?

Matthew read my expression. "It takes a little getting used to in here. We have no weight, so we can jump real high. You'll get the hang of it."

"If we have no weight, what holds us to the ground?" Lilly asked.

"The dark water. It's everywhere. When there isn't much of that stuff in the air, I can jump so high. It's like I'm flying."

Matthew sprung into the darkness. He ascended higher and higher until he too disappeared over the edge of the gear.

Lilly nudged me. "Well, go on."

I pushed off the ground with all of my strength. More strength than was needed. I shot through the air and zipped right past the gear where the group stood waiting. Some of the kids laughed and pointed as I zoomed by.

I plummeted toward a gear at least twenty feet below me. It made no sense, but I flapped my arms as hard as I could and cinched my eyes shut. I felt the blackness leak from my pores as I fell, speckling the sky. The anticipated deadly impact never came. Instead, I landed lightly in front of the group. I opened my eyes. Most of the kids were still giggling.

"Let's get moving," Redmond commanded. The group followed him off the edge of the gear. Will hung back.

"Got a little overzealous there, huh Caleb?" Will smirked.

"It's not easy to control." I wiped the specks of dark water off my arms.

"Yet Lilly jumped it just right. Like a pro," said Matthew. She smiled proudly.

"Don't worry, Caleb. You'll get the hang of it." Will walked toward the ledge. "You gotta get that fear under control there, buddy." He pointed to the pool of darkness at my feet. "That stuff will lead Darkwater right to us."

"I wonder how high NBA players can jump after they die." Matthew dropped off the side of the gear.

"What in the heck is an NBA?" Will asked as he

stepped off the ledge.

The journey was the wildest of my life, or, I guess, my afterlife. We jumped and glided over gears and jagged platforms. The whole group stayed far away from the darkest areas. All of the thrill I should've felt became a jolt of terror every time a shadow slithered out of a corner or a blob of blackness writhed toward us as we ran.

The gears pulsed under our feet to the rhythm of time in the outside world. What was happening out there? What would happen when they found our bodies, slumped on the floor of the museum? My mom. Her face as I left. The pain I'd caused her. Those cruel words were the last I would ever say to her.

"I love your hair," Grace said to Lilly. "It's so pretty." Lilly smiled back at Grace and nodded a stiff thank you.

We glided to the ground and the group fell silent. A patch of open area lay before us, the dark tower in plain view, wobbling like black Jell-o. I forced myself to look away from it.

We crept quietly, Mr. Redmond put his finger to his mouth and tiptoed across the brass ground. We followed. Shadows in the corner shook and dripped out toward us. The tendrils of nightmare crept along behind us.

"Guys?" I tapped Will on the shoulder. The

trickles of dark water blobbed together into a barking Doberman, its eyes oozing with vapor, sharp grey teeth snapping at our heels. A little boy screamed.

"He knows we're here," Will yelled. "Faster!"

Lilly and I followed the mass of frightened children. We hurtled to a nearby gear, but it was too late. Dark water surged toward us like a flash flood. The gear we stood upon clicked forward one notch, knocking Lilly and me to the ground. I pulled her up as the dark water rushed toward us. It reached out for us as we leaped from the ledge. The air whistled past our faces as we landed on the large gear below us. The dark water poured down from the dizzying heights above and splashed to the ground behind. We ran as fast as we could, catching up to the group.

"Lilly, Caleb, to the front," Will hollered. I gave Lilly a bewildered look as the frantic children made a gap through their running formation and beckoned us to run ahead.

"He's right. It's you Darkwater's after," Anna said. I looked down at the orange glow burning in my chest. Pure terror took over Lilly's eyes.

"Go!" I shouted at her. She shot out in front of me and we ran into the center of the crowd.

The dark water wrapped around Grace's ankle. She fell to her stomach, her pale blue eyes wide with terror.

"Grace!" Will yelled. He stopped in his tracks and dashed toward her.

"Dang it, Will!" Anna followed him.

"Help!" screamed the little girl. She tried to pull away but the darkness yanked her into it completely. Even from very near the front of the group, her screams rang loud in my ears as she was enveloped.

"Grace!" Will shouted again. Without hesitation, he dove into the blackness.

"Keep running! Leave them. They'll be okay," Mr. Redmond shouted. The dark water stopped pursuing us, but now it had gulped up Anna as well.

"Look ahead, not behind," Matthew said.

I knew I should listen to him, but I couldn't ignore the howls of a little girl who couldn't have been more than seven years old. I couldn't just leave her there. I had already failed so many people. Lilly, my mom. My dad. I couldn't let anyone else get hurt because of me.

I spun around and took off running toward the billowing wave of darkness.

"Caleb, don't do it. He'll get your Glow," Matthew yelled.

Lilly turned to follow me, but Matthew grabbed her hand. "Don't go. You still have a chance!" She stood still for a moment and then turned and followed Matthew.

I was glad. She'd already suffered enough because

of my mistakes.

The darkness reached out before I was even close to it. It wrapped around me like a straitjacket. Will, Anna, and Grace were tossed around mercilessly, surrounded by terrible images made from the blackness. Grace screamed as masses of fat black wasps swarmed her, landing all over her face and arms. She swatted and cried as they buzzed louder and louder. Anna wrestled against the water, wrapped tight in the darkness, the strands holding her arms close to her sides, crushing her in its powerful grip. A massive snake coiled around Will. It put its fanged face right up to Will's and flicked its forked tongue at his nose. Will struggled but the snake held him tighter, hovering around his neck, ready to strike.

I was clamped in a wheelchair. I couldn't move. A familiar squealing sound filled the air. My dad moved toward me. His own wheelchair rolled him closer and closer. His flesh sagged and his eyes stared ahead, vacant, unresponsive. I tried to wriggle free from the bonds that held me in the chair, but I couldn't. Screams belted out all around me. My father didn't move. He just sat and stared. I tried to look away from him, but I couldn't. He was alive and he was dead. I thrashed against the blackness and it gripped me tighter.

My father split into a vapory mist and then re-formed as the oozing man in a steel grey suit. His long arched neck craned to get a better look at me. He moved closer as the drips of dark water slithered over his dull, white eyeballs.

I'd been a fool. I couldn't help Will, Anna, or Grace.

I was about to lose my only chance to live again.

CHAPTER

He reached out for me, his fingers writhing as they entered my chest and wrapped around my Glow. I couldn't move. Fear completely paralyzed me.

This was it. He had my Glow clenched in his stringy fingers.

His grip slackened, fingers spread.

"Let them go," came a voice through the surge. Darkwater released his grip on my Glow. For a moment, the mass of liquid fear opened. In the clearing, Mr. Redmond stood quaking behind the dark figure.

"You!" hissed Darkwater. I trembled from head to foot. Mr. Redmond stepped to the right. Something was different about how he moved.

"Let them go," he repeated. And still, something was wrong. The way he bobbed up and down reminded me of something. What was it?

"I will send you to your death." The dark water loosened from around my limbs.

"Only if you can catch me." Mr. Redmond took off running. The waves reformed and rolled away in pursuit. Darkwater remained, standing before me. He looked toward Redmond, then back at me. Finally, with a hiss, he melted into the crashing waves of water and flowed off.

I lay gasping. I coughed and coughed. Black ooze filled my mouth as I heaved. The newly formed dark water flowed off to find its master.

And that's when I remembered.

My ghost! The one I'd made to prank Blake. Redmond's movements when he stood before Darkwater were like my helium balloon ghost. Or maybe a puppet. Or anything that was supposed to look convincing but was actually completely fake. Everything from the way his mouth moved to how he ran was overexaggerated, like a marionette.

He'd appeared just when I'd needed him most and then slipped between a stack of gears, the dark water trailing behind. He'd risked his own life to save mine. A perfect move to win my trust.

Too perfect.

I wasn't sure what Redmond was up to. Maybe he

was a control freak who enjoyed making the kids follow his little rules. Maybe he was in on it with Darkwater, using the rules to keep us from finding a way out on our own. He'd had more than a hundred years to find an escape route. If he was actually trying, he wasn't doing a very good job.

But I was very sure Redmond wasn't the person that led Darkwater away from me. That was some kind of illusion. A prank.

And no one pranks the master-prankster.

"Grace? Are you okay? Grace?" Will knelt next to her.

"I'm okay. I'm sorry. I couldn't keep up." Grace's whole body shivered.

Anna glared at me. "You need to be more careful. He only came after us because he wants your Glow. You almost gave him exactly what he wanted."

"I couldn't let. . . I couldn't. . . ." Realization washed over me. This had all been a trap set by Darkwater. My new friends had been the bait, and I'd leaped in head-first again.

"You're lucky he wants Mr. Redmond more than he wants your Glow," Will said.

"Mr. Redmond saved me before," Grace said. "He's my hero."

They were all in with Mr. Redmond. He had them

doing whatever he said. What did he really want?

"Come on. Darkwater still knows where we are. I'll take you to the hiding spot." Anna stood up. I scanned the ground for any sign of the dark water but it was gone; not a trace of it left.

We ran for what seemed like hours. Although I no longer had a body, I was so emotionally drained I could barely keep going. Anna and Will didn't look much better, but they put on a good show for Grace. The brave little girl kept running, even with black tears still running down her cheeks. Her arms and face were speckled with the darkness.

Will did his best to get her to stop crying. The goofy faces he made at her had no impact, but his tripping and falling while trying to do them got a few laughs between the tears.

We kept going.

In a dark spot, right next to the rounded metal wall of level two, we skidded to a halt.

"We've almost made it, Gracie. Five big jumps and we're there," Anna said. Grace didn't look too thrilled about jumping up the metal gears that clinked together above us.

"What if he's already up there? What if he's waiting for us?" Grace asked, her voice hoarse from screaming.

"We can't think like that, Grace," Anna said. "Mr.

Redmond has always protected us. If this place isn't safe, then no place is safe."

"I don't think there are any safe places here. I want to go home. I want to see my mom and dad." Grace wiped her eyes.

"That home is long gone, Grace. They've all moved on, without us. Remember what Mr. Redmond told us. We're here for a reason. We just need to stick together and we'll find out what that reason is," Will said.

Grace nodded, her lips tight with concentration.

We leaped up and up, from platform to platform, until we landed on the ridge of a large gear, about the size of a football field to me, although I'm sure it was less than an inch across. The gear had long, narrow beams that led from the outer ridge to the inner circle. Anna, Will, and I balanced carefully across them. I tried not to look down, but accidentally glanced that way twice. Below me was a mass of spinning wheels with sharp teeth colliding. One misstep and I would be right in the middle of all of that. I had to remind myself it would probably have no effect, since I was already dead.

The cluster of children was huddled close on the center ring of the gear. There was an immediate reaction from them when they saw us crossing the beams. They ran to Will, Grace, and Anna.

Finally, it was time to rest. I was exhausted. Not the

same type of tired I felt when I was alive. More like I'd been wiped out emotionally. Lilly and Matthew sat far away from the others. She scowled at me as I stumbled closer.

"You are an idiot," Lilly said.

"I know." I plopped down beside her. Will, Anna, and Grace joined us, forming a small circle of bodies.

Grace stole several glances in our direction, her eyelids heavy, before she curled up on the ground and fell asleep.

"I owe both of you an apology." Anna stared at the ground. "I'm sorry for what I said about not helping you."

"It's not a big deal," Lilly said. "We're sorry we caused so much trouble."

Guilt washed through me, streaming out of my pores.

Will smacked me in the back of the head. "Cut that out. Whatever you're feeling. It could lead Darkwater right to us."

"You said stuff about getting taken?" I stretched my legs out in front of me and tried to calm down. "What actually happens when someone gets taken? What does that mean?"

Will checked Grace, examining her quiet face. Then he turned back toward us. "When someone breaks too many rules, the water comes for them and takes them away to their second death."

Lilly leaned in. "Second death?"

"Yeah. We never see them again," Will whispered. "It's happened to about twelve people since we came here."

Lilly leaned in. "Who made up all of these rules?"

"I don't know." Will scratched his chin. "Darkwater, I guess."

Anna leaned back on her arms. "Before we came, there was a woman here. She was beautiful and so was her voice. I still miss her."

Will draped his elbows over his knees. "Her name was Afton Wallace. She was taken while she was singing a song. Since then, no one dares to sing. Rule One."

"I saw the dark water come for her. It wrapped around her like a fist and dragged her away from us. We never saw her again." Anna's head drooped as she finished her story.

"After Afton, we lost Reverend Sheridan. He told us to pray for deliverance. After he was taken, we don't pray anymore. Rule Two."

"What about Mr. Redmond? Where did he come from? Was he on the train with you?" I asked.

"No. Mr. Redmond was the first person to be trapped here. He was so good at hiding from Darkwater he avoided being taken for years, even before we got here. He's been our guide and guardian pretty much ever since the train wreck," Will said.

"What do you know about him? About his life before all this?"

Matthew leaned toward me. "I know you should listen to him, Caleb. He's a good man. He tried to help me when I first came here, but I didn't listen. That's how I lost my Glow." Matthew pointed to my orange chest.

Matthew had been trapped here for the shortest amount of time besides Lilly and me and he already completely trusted Redmond.

"I went to your funeral, Matthew," Lilly said in a whisper.

"You did?"

"Yes."

"Were my parents there?"

"Yes."

"They went? After everything I said? After everything I did?"

"Remember, Matthew. That wasn't you who did those things to them," Anna reminded him.

"It just makes me feel better to know they came. Maybe they forgave me. Maybe they knew. . . ." Matthew trailed off.

Will nodded at him. "Darkwater reached into his

spirit with his hand and pulled the Glow right out of him. Then, Darkwater took Matthew's Glow into the outside world and used it to take possession of his body."

"He did horrible things with it," Matthew said, shuddering. "He sometimes shows me what I did when he was in my body, the pain he caused my family. The awful things I said and did."

We sat in silence for a moment. I stared down at my glowing chest, a small ember of hope burning within. If I still had my Glow, I could still reconnect with my body. If I could get out of here, somehow, I could be alive again.

Lilly stared at her own Glow, maybe thinking the same thing.

"So, if you two want to keep those Glows, you'll need to follow all of the rules." Anna held up her fist and began counting off fingers. "One: No singing. Two: No praying. Three: No contact. Four: Don't look at the dark tower."

"We've got to find a way out of here," I whispered.

"I would've never thought that being dead could be so exhausting." Lilly scooted back and settled on the ground.

"You're not dead yet," Will said.

"There's always hope." Anna nodded. "At least, that's what Afton always told me."

And where was she? Not exactly inspiring. We had to find a way past Darkwater. I wouldn't be able to do it alone, but could I convince anyone else to disobey Redmond and go with me?

Lilly curled up on the floor. It only took seconds for her to fall asleep. She was still super-pretty, even though she was dead. The orange glow grew brighter in my chest.

"Oh, you like her." Will chuckled in my ear.

"No, I don't," I replied, almost automatically. To protest was useless. It was obvious how I felt for Lilly. It was like my Glow had gone nuclear.

"It's okay, Anna and I like each other too."

"You do?" I asked. Anna nodded her head.

I glanced back at Lilly. She was completely asleep. I turned back to Will and Anna, the reflection of my Glow emblazoned on the metal floor in front of me.

"Problem is, I don't think she likes me back. I'm kind of an idiot."

"Oh, you never know what's going on in a girl's heart," Anna said. "I didn't let on that I liked Will for a long time."

"A very long time," Will agreed. The two smiled at each other again.

"Is that a problem, though? I mean, can dead people be... uh, you know, in love?"

"You learn pretty quickly love is a lot bigger than life and death." Anna touched Will's hand with her slender fingers, cautiously. Will smiled at her. She pulled them away.

A little bit of hope crept back into my soul. The gears clicked into place again.

I let go. I emptied my brain of all thoughts and emotions. No fear. No sadness. My ghost body went slack. In seconds, I fell asleep.

CHAPTER 15

I was in a dusty room, a muffled sound in the background.

My hand! I could see my real hand!

I tried to move it, but I couldn't. The sound was coming from a person. Sobbing.

My hands were cold, and so was the room. The person next to me became very still. Slowly, he turned his head toward me.

"Caleb? Are you there?"

It was Austin.

"Austin," I tried to scream, but my lips wouldn't move. I could see him, his face right in mine, his eyes wide.

"You *are* here." Relief spread across his face.

"Can you hear me?" I tried to shout. My body didn't respond. I concentrated with all of my might to try to move my arm or twitch my lip. Nothing. Whatever was happening, I was not connected to my body.

"I can hear you," Austin said. "Where are you? Is Lilly with you?"

"Yes," I answered. Austin could hear me! He wasn't lying about being able to sense spirits.

"It was a trap, Austin. We're trapped in the watch."

"Wait. You guys are in the watch?"

"Yes. Well, our spirits are anyway."

"Hold on. I think I feel Lilly's presence now, too. I'm gonna go talk to her."

"Wait! Austin!" He walked away from me and knelt down in the shadows. Lilly was there, slumped against the wall. For a moment, I felt sick. She looked like she was dead, her eyes open but blank, her mouth hanging limply. She reminded me of. . . .

I pushed the thought from my mind.

Austin knew stuff about this kind of weirdness. Maybe he had answers. I tried to make my head move to get a better view, but it wouldn't budge. It felt so heavy, like a massive boulder. I wasn't strong enough. I could never be strong enough.

I couldn't see Hillary, but I heard her crying.

"Lilly? Can you hear me?" Austin said. There was no response.

"Yeah, I was just talking to him," Austin said. I

could hear Austin, but I couldn't hear Lilly. What was going on?

"I need you to calm down, Lilly. We'll figure this out. Try to get yourself under control. I'm gonna go back and talk to Caleb." He patted her still body on the shoulder and stumbled back to me.

"Dude, I told you not to touch that watch."

"Yeah, well, we touched it, Austin, so that advice is no longer helpful."

"Sarcasm isn't going to help you out of this either, Caleb."

I wanted to kill him. I didn't need a lecture right now. I needed help.

"Okay, you win. We shouldn't have touched the watch. Lesson learned. Now tell us how to get out of here and reattach to our bodies."

"You can't reattach to your bodies," Austin said.

"Yes, we can. The other people in the watch told us we can. As long as we have our Glows."

"I don't know what you're talking about. Glows? What I do know is that you aren't really here. You're still trapped. Your consciousness is here, but not your full spirit."

"Austin, you idiot. I'm here right now. I can see you."

"I know, Caleb, but you aren't here. Your presence

is so weak. What was the last thing that happened in the watch before you came here?"

"Let's see. Uh . . . we were chased by black water that tried to steal our souls, then we jumped up a bunch of gears to hide from it. Last thing I remember, I laid down. I guess I fell asleep."

Austin nodded his head.

"So, your spirit is asleep and your consciousness came here?"

"I . . . I . . . guess so."

"Whoa! Spirits can sleep? That's cool! I never knew. . . ."

"Austin! We need help! There's this guy in the watch who wants to take over our bodies. He's hunting us."

"Wait a minute! Is Matthew Bradford in there with you?" Austin asked.

"Yeah. That's what happened to him. This Dark-water guy took over his body and made him do crazy things. Then he killed the body and went back into the watch."

"Why would a spirit hunt other spirits?" Austin's forehead crinkled.

"I don't know why. He's insane? The kids think he's the devil." It was such a strain to talk to him, like I had to focus every bit of what I was in his direction just to

153

whisper into the air around him.

"What kids?"

"The ones from the train wreck. They've been trapped in here for ages."

"Holy crap! You're in there with the kids that died in the Great Train Wreck of 1856! This is incredible!"

If only I could've raised my hand and smacked Austin upside the head. "So. I'm pretty much dead here, and you're like, 'That's incredible!'"

Austin's eyes lit up. "A possessed object inhabited by a ghost who preys on the fears of other ghosts. Creedy wrote about these kinds of spirits. They're called. . . uh. . . wait a second. . . ." Austin whipped out his cell phone and slid his finger over the face. "They're called. . ."

"Dude, I don't care about Ed Creedy or his weird website. Get me out of here!"

Austin continued to scroll. "I can't get you out, Caleb. You have to do that. If you're going to have a chance at escaping, you need to know as much as you can about this ghost."

"There's gotta be something you can do!"

Austin paused mid-scroll. "Matthew Bradford."

"Yep. He's here and he's dead. We're going to be dead too unless you do something to help us!"

"No. Listen!" He looked directly into my eyes.

"You said Darkwater came out of the watch to take over Matthew Bradford's body?"

"Yeah, that's what I said. So what?"

"So, there's gotta be an exit somewhere. There's a way in and a way out. You need to find it. You need to get back out."

"How? Where would it be?" I felt myself fading. I hung on to the feeling of physicality. The beat of my heart. The breath in my lungs.

Austin pointed at his phone screen. "It's a Dreadmonger, Caleb! I found it! The ghost is a Dreadmonger."

"Austin, I can't hold on. I'm fading." My vision became blurry, Austin just a blob of grey in front of me.

"Dreadmongers feed off of fear, Caleb. He gets stronger the more afraid you are!" His voice was more and more muffled.

"Austin!" How could I stop being afraid? This was literally life or death.

"You have to think like a Dreadmonger, Caleb. If you can outsmart him, you can escape."

I needed more information. I needed to know more about Darkwater. I needed to know more about Redmond. I shouted out the names I'd heard as I slipped away from Austin.

"Darkwater! Redmond!" One more name popped into my head. The second prisoner in the watch. "Afton

Wallace!"

"You're drifting away, Caleb. Remember what I said: Think like a Dreadmonger!" Austin's voice faded to a slight muffle as I slipped back into consciousness inside the watch.

I opened my eyes slowly. The dull silver ceiling was the first thing I saw. I sat up. Lilly was still asleep. Will and Anna were both awake, staring at me.

"What?" I asked.

"You were talking," Will said.

"More like shouting," Anna corrected.

"Yeah, shouting."

"I was having a dream?" My heart sunk. If it wasn't real, then I hadn't really spoken to Austin. The things we talked about might all be a lie, just solutions my mind created to make me feel better, but nothing that would work.

"No," Anna said. "We don't dream here. We just rest."

"No one dreams here?" I asked.

"No," Will said. "But you were shouting names."

"I need to know if it was real." I ran over to Lilly and pushed on her cold, still body.

"Lilly? Lilly?" I shook her until she sat up, blinking at me in confusion.

"Oh no," she said.

"Were you there, Lilly? Did you talk to Austin?"

"Yes. Were you really there, too?"

"Yes! This is great! We got through."

Will scratched his head. "Who's Austin?"

Lilly's stood up. "Austin is our friend on the outside of the watch. He saw us get sucked in. He can still talk to us even though he's alive.

"Whoa! That's amazing!" Will's eyes went wide.

I turned back to Lilly. "What did Austin tell you?"

"He said Darkwater's something called a Dread-monger."

"Yep. Did he tell you anything else?"

"No. You woke me up."

Will's mouth tightened into a straight line. "A Dreadmonger? What's that?"

Lilly dusted herself off out of habit. "It's a ghost. A ghost that feeds on fear."

"That sounds pretty far-fetched."

"More far-fetched than Darkwater being the devil?" I asked.

"Yes, Caleb." Anna folded her arms. "You've seen him. I'm pretty sure he *is* the Devil."

My brain was piecing things together, trying to follow Austin's advice to think like a Dreadmonger. This place surrounded us with fear and guilt. Hope was basically outlawed. Banned by Redmond's rules. The rules that kept us afraid and in hiding. The rules that kept us from searching for a way out.

"I know what I need to do now."

"And what's that?" Lilly asked.

"Austin says if there's an entrance, then there's an exit. He said Darkwater must know about it if he left the watch to claim Matthew Bradford's body. He has always known about it."

"We've been trapped in here for so long, Caleb," Anna said. "We've been all around this place. I've never seen anything that looked like an exit."

"What about Level Three?" Will asked, his lip curling recklessly. "You know, the big hole in the casing where the winding dial is inserted?"

"Will, you know perfectly well that it's sealed. Darkwater has it blocked off. You've been there at least a thousand times," Anna replied.

"It just seems like, if the light can get through there, why couldn't we?"

Anna's nose crinkled. "The last time you tried that, you couldn't break through the seal and then Darkwater came after us. It was too close. No more risks!"

I stood and took a few steps toward the edge, staring out into the ticking world before me. "It wouldn't be in an obvious place. We need to think like a Dreadmonger. Where would you put an exit? Where would you put it if you didn't want anyone to go near it?" I pointed in the direction of the tower, now blocked from our view by a curtain of churning gears. Everyone followed my gaze, but looked away, quickly.

"You're talking about the dark tower? You can't even look at it without being attacked," Will stated.

I turned back toward them. "That's my point. The tower rises through all three levels of the watch. Dark-water's rule is a distraction." I paced back toward the edge, running a hand through my hair. "He feeds off our fear. He keeps us afraid of our only way out."

"You think there's an exit in there?" Anna asked.

I nodded. "Yes."

Will held his chin in his palm, lost in thought.

"I have nothing to lose, Anna." I stepped closer to her. "If I don't find a way out, I'm dead."

Lily stomped her foot. "I am too, Caleb. Don't forget about that."

"We've been here for so long, Caleb. We wanted to get out, too. We never could." Will raised an eyebrow. "We never found a way past the dark water. Only Mr. Redmond has escaped from it and he's had some pretty close calls."

How could I tell them about Mr. Redmond's stunt double and get them to believe it? They'd trusted him for so long.

Anna pointed toward a huddle of sleeping children. "If you're wondering, he did make it back. He's sleeping now. He arrived a few minutes after you fell asleep."

Amid the still bodies was a larger one. The real Mr. Redmond. Not the puppet I'd seen before. Even though he wasn't moving, I could see the difference. The other Redmond had been more grey, more transparent.

Had he been made of dark water?

"Have you ever noticed anything strange about Mr. Redmond?"

"He takes care of us. He's a great man." Anna turned toward him and smiled.

I bit my lip. "I'm not sure he's what he says he is."

Anna's hands went to her hips. "Excuse me, Caleb?"

Will shook his head. "Now look here. You've only just arrived. We know Mr. Redmond better than you do."

"Are you sure about that?" I locked eyes with Will.

Lilly elbowed me in the stomach. "Caleb!"

"I think the rules of this place were made to keep you afraid."

Anna shook her finger at me. "That's what you're getting at. Trying to find reasons to disregard the rules. And coming after Mr. Redmond of all people to do it. I know you want to get out of here, but breaking the rules puts us all in danger. This isn't just about you. Every time Darkwater comes for the children. . . ."

Will slammed his fist into his palm, his eyes blazing. "Isn't that just it, though? If Caleb is right, Darkwater gets stronger when we're afraid. He wants us living in fear. If we don't make some changes, nothing's gonna change."

"Will, please don't do anything stupid again. You're the only reason I can stand it here."

Will stamped his foot. "That's what I'm talking about, Anna. We shouldn't have to be here. We should've moved on. We don't belong in hell. And we sure don't belong here."

I stepped between them. "I don't want to get anyone else involved, but I'm not sure there's another way. I'm going to the tower, but I need some kind of distraction to lure Darkwater away so I can get in. Do you have any ideas?"

"That's crazy. You'll be taken. You'll be lost forever," Anna said.

· "What should I do, Anna? Stay here and run for a hundred years just like you? Aren't you tired of running yet? Aren't you ready to fight?"

"You sound just like Fredrick did," Anna replied. "And Matthew before he lost his Glow."

"What you don't understand is that Darkwater is only strong because we feed him. He's only strong because we're afraid." I walked toward the edge of the gear, carefully avoiding the groups of sleeping children. Mr. Redmond was still asleep.

I peered over the edge. "We need to stop being afraid."

"That's easy to say but hard to do," Anna replied.

"Not always," said a tiny voice from behind me.

Grace sat up from where she lay. "I used to be afraid of the dark, but I'm not anymore. Daddy taught me to just close my eyes. He told me if I close my eyes, before I know it, it'll be morning, and I'll wake up safe, like I do every morning. Daddy said the more you do something, the less afraid you become. At first, I was still scared, but after a week or so, I wasn't scared anymore."

Lilly stepped closer to the little girl. "You're very brave."

"Yeah. I know." She stood proud, her curly ringlets framing her wide grin.

"And she's right," Will said, "and so is Caleb. We've been running for too long. It's time for us to start facing our fears."

"You don't really believe we can do this? Do you?" Anna's angry glare darted from Will to me and back again.

"Who knows? All I know is Lilly and Caleb still have a chance to live. Maybe we'll get out of here, too, while we're at it."

"But Will, what about getting taken?" Anna moved closer to him.

Will stared right into her eyes. "I don't know what happens next, but I know we can't stay here."

Anna nodded slowly. Will moved closer to her. "We can't be afraid. Even of losing each other. If we are, he wins."

"You're going to help him, then?" Anna's voice was almost a whisper, her eyes staring back into his.

"Yes." Will smiled and turned to me. "Caleb, if you're planning on breakin' some rules, count me in."

Anna scooted forward too.

"Count *us* in," she said.

CHAPTER 16

Grace stomped her foot and stuck out her bottom lip.

"I'm coming too!"

"Gracie, it's dangerous. Just stay at camp and we'll be back soon," Will pleaded.

"No. I'm coming."

"We're just going to scout things out. It's probably going to be really boring," I said. That tactic worked with my seven year old cousin when he'd stayed with us last summer and wanted to follow me everywhere. It didn't work on Grace.

"If you don't let me come, I'll wake everybody up. I'll tell them that you're gonna break more rules," Grace threatened.

I stared her down. A little seven-year-old ghost thinking she could tell me what to do? No way.

She stared right back at me.

Okay. Never mind.

"Fine," Anna said. "You can come. But you have to do everything I say. Promise?"

Grace jumped up and down. "I promise!"

"Shhhhhhh!" We all shushed in unison. She clamped her hands over her mouth and looked around. No one had heard. Mr. Redmond's arm twitched and then lay still.

Will motioned to us to move in closer.

"If we try to get into the fortress, Darkwater will stop us. I have an idea that might buy us some time."

"What are you thinking?" Anna asked.

"I've done my share of scouting, even when I'm not supposed to. Mr. Redmond has always told us that it's safer here on level two than on level one or level three."

"Have you been to level three?" Lilly asked.

"Yup. Anna and I have risked a few trips down to level three," Will said. An awkward smile spread over Anna's face.

"What's down there?" I asked.

"Not a lot. It's very open. There's nowhere to hide. If Darkwater senses us down there, he'll probably come after us. I can lead him on a wild goose chase while Caleb and Lilly sneak into the fortress and try to find a way out."

"What will I be doing?" Grace asked.

"You and Anna will stay near the fortress to help protect Caleb and Lilly from Darkwater in case he comes after them."

"I'm not dumb, Will. I know what you're doing," Grace said. "You're just keeping me out of the way. I can help. I'm not afraid."

"I know, Gracie. I am afraid, though. I'm afraid for you. If you are safe with Anna, then I'll be able to focus on leading the dark water away from Caleb and Lilly. Does that make sense?"

Grace gave him a sulky pout, but conceded a nod. Anna didn't look too fond of the plan.

"Alright. It's now or never." Will leaped from the platform and disappeared into the darkness below. Anna followed him and then Lilly. Grace was next. I surveyed the camp one final time. Mr. Redmond lay still surrounded by the children. He tossed fitfully, his face scrunching into a sneer.

The children slept peacefully. So quiet. So still. As if they were dead.

They were dead.

And so was I if I didn't do something.

I leaped off the edge of the gear just as it jolted to mark the passing of another minute. As I fell slowly, an orange light glimmered through the fog of darkness.

Lilly. I plunged through the last of the mists and landed at her side.

"Whatever happens, Lilly and Caleb need to stay away from Darkwater," Will said.

"I'm not afraid of him." I tried to sound brave but my voice cracked.

Will shook his head. "You have the most to lose, Caleb. You and Lilly."

Anna's green and brown eyes bloomed with affection for Will. Guilt seeped into me again. What if this plan didn't work? What if I was wrong? Tiny drips of dark water peeked out from my pores.

Grace smacked my arm. "Caleb! No fear!"

I smiled at her. "Yep. No fear!" The beads of dark water faded into mist.

We took off. I missed the feeling of footfalls on the ground, the burn of my muscles, and the trickle of sweat, but the exhilaration of speed was something that almost made up for it.

We raced down the staircase of tremendous gears. I glanced over my shoulder. There was no one behind us. Our escape had been timed just right. Anna and Grace were behind me. Grace kept up like a champ despite her short legs. Will led the way. Lilly was right behind him. She didn't look back.

The path to level three was through a tight space

between the gears. Will looked down into the depths below. A blood-red light shone upon his face.

"We used to be afraid to go down here. Some kids thought it was hell. Mr. Redmond told us that it's not hell, but it is dangerous. Like I said before, very few places to hide."

"Will and I like to come here sometimes. At certain times of day it's very beautiful," Anna said.

"If you think anything in this place is beautiful, you've definitely been stuck here too long." I stepped to the ledge as Will slipped into the darkness.

Lilly glared at me. "They're risking everything for us. The least you could do is be polite."

"I thought I *was* being polite."

"Stop being a jerk."

A jerk? Moi? Normally, a string of sarcasm would've flowed off of my tongue that would have infuriated Gandhi.

Not this time. I had nothing. I stood silenced by her as she slipped down into the dark shaft. A red glare flashed from below as she went. I followed.

I slid through the gears into the darkness.

There wasn't much in level three. The ground itself was just metal. The ceiling, on the other hand, was a whole different story.

A golden wheel with delicately shaped spokes

hung from above like a massive chandelier. It ticked in a perfect rhythm. Mesmerizing. I stood, gawking, trying to follow the ornate patterns etched into the metal.

But it wasn't just the wheel that was breathtaking. A beam of light shot through a large hole behind us. Just above the wheel, two massive red stones glittered in the shadows, moving up and down, like they were on a teeter-totter. As each gem hit the light, red blotches of color danced on the walls, floor, and ceiling.

Will, Anna, Grace, and Lilly stood staring at the light show in awe. Lilly's Glow shone brightly.

"It's only like this at certain times of the day, when the light from outside is shining directly on the hole for the winding key." Anna reached her arms out and let a blur of vivid color wash over her body, basking in it like a sunbeam.

Dark water oozed around the keyhole, covering it completely, but even its murky blackness couldn't stop the perfect flow of light from the outside.

Will stepped next to me. "I tried it, Caleb. It's covered in that gunk. Didn't get anywhere."

I nodded. "It's too obvious. Of course he'd have strong defenses here."

"You think the tower will be different?"

A splash of red lit up the floor below me. "He doesn't want you looking at it. He's hiding something.

It's gotta be his weakness."

"I've never seen it like this before." Grace's eyes were wide, reflections of red dancing in them.

"Mr. Redmond said that bringing the group here would generate too much good feelings. He said Darkwater would sense it immediately and come after us." Will smiled wide.

"That hasn't stopped us from sneaking away and coming down here every once in a while." Anna winked at Will. I cringed a little. I really didn't want to think about ghosts making out.

"How come the watch is always running?" Lilly asked.

"Not really sure. I've always guessed Darkwater has some way to wind it. The main spring here just needs a few turns and the watch will run for about three or four hours." Will pointed to a bit of exposed coil behind the massive wheel above us.

"When do you think Darkwater will come for us?"

"I don't know." Will stared into the darkness, searching for any sign of movement. "But we need to be ready."

"Will, can we talk alone?"

"I don't know if this is a good time."

"It may be the only chance we get. Come on." Anna grabbed his arm. Will rolled his eyes and followed. They sat down on the ground about thirty or forty feet away from us.

"It's so beautiful." Lilly gazed above us, still hypnotized by the light show.

"Yeah," I said, "Will was right."

Lilly glanced at me. "I'm sorry I was angry with you back there, Caleb."

"You don't have to be. I deserved it," I replied.

She shook her head. "I'm trying my hardest not to be afraid and it's so hard."

"It's hard for me, too."

"Me too," said Grace.

I jumped. I almost forgot she was still with us.

"I thought you weren't afraid of anything, Grace." Lilly sat down on the floor and patted the ground beside her.

Grace shrugged and plopped down next to her. "Not much, but some things."

"Do you think it would help if we all talked about our fears?" Lilly asked.

"I can go first." Grace bounced up and down with excitement.

"Go for it." As long as it wasn't me. Grace glanced side to side, like she was about to reveal a well-guarded secret.

"Okay. When I was just a little girl, something

171

happened to me. Something bad. I found a wasps' nest. I didn't know what it was, so I threw a rock at it to get it down from a tree branch. I hit it real hard. Parts of it broke off and scattered everywhere. Then I saw a cloud rise off the broken parts. There were thousands of wasps, and they attacked me. I ran and screamed and swatted at them, but I was too far away from my house, so no one heard me. I got stung so many times. My daddy finally heard me screaming, and he saved me. He ran right into those wasps and picked me up. I was kicking and hollering, but he ran me away. My arms and legs were so swollen from all of those stings. The doctor said I coulda died from them. Since then, I've been scared of wasps."

Grace shivered as she finished her story. Black essence dripped from the pores of her arms and slid to the ground.

"I don't know if talking about our fears is such a good idea." I tried to stomp the black blobs, but they zipped around my feet and flitted away.

"I think it is," Lilly said, "but we need to come up with ways to overcome our fears. Your dad saved you, right Grace? How did you feel when he was around you?"

"I always felt safe around Daddy. He was so strong, he could whoop up on a grizzly bear." Grace's shivering

172

stopped at the mention of her dad. So did the flow of fear from her body.

"That's what we need." Lilly clapped her hands together. "We need good thoughts to help us battle our fears. Anything that makes us feel better when we're afraid."

"It worked, Lilly. When I think of Daddy, I'm not afraid anymore!"

"That's wonderful, Grace! Now let's help Caleb. What are you afraid of, Caleb?"

Lilly kind of knew who I was afraid of. She had seen him many times by now. I wondered what it looked like to her as I cowered before a shriveled man in a wheelchair. Just the thought of him sent shivers through my spirit. Black essence leaked from my body.

Grace yanked on my arm. "Tell us, Caleb. It'll help."

"I'm not afraid." My denial was pathetic since fear was literally bleeding out of me.

"Come on, Caleb. Don't be all macho about this." Lilly leaned forward.

"You're afraid of drowning. That's obvious," I blurted, hoping to get the attention off of me.

Lilly sighed, well aware of what I was doing. She went with it anyway.

"I was in the first grade. My family was at a beach in New Jersey. My sister and I were out playing in the

173

waves. She told me I was out too far. I told her to shove it. Then, a huge wave crashed down on me. I felt like I was being trampled to death. Water wrapped all around me. I couldn't move. I couldn't breathe. I thrashed and struggled. It did no good at all. I was at the bottom of the ocean, sand against my back. As I lay there, my lungs burning for air, I realized I wasn't coming back up. It was like an invisible hand was holding me down. I felt the sand settle around me like dirt being pitched into my grave. I blacked out. The next thing I remember, I was lying on the beach, coughing up salt water."

"That sounds awful." Grace's already large eyes were even larger.

"My father saved me. He dove in and pulled me out."

"Do you feel better when you think about him, like me?"

"No, actually, I don't."

"Why not?"

"Well Grace, my father left us last year. He's gone. I never had nightmares about drowning when he lived with us, even right after it happened. After he left, though, I have them every night."

"Where did he go?"

"He went away and married another woman."

"My ma would've beat my daddy senseless if he did

something like that." Grace pounded her fist into her hand.

"So, I don't know how to make my fear go away." Lilly's head hung low.

"So, your daddy saved you, and now he's gone." Grace rubbed her chin. "So you're scared because you feel like there's no one to save you."

Lilly smiled. "You really are a very smart girl."

"I know that," said Grace.

"So my secret's out. What's yours?" Lilly turned to me.

No one else to hide behind. I tried to think of some way to change the subject, but nothing came to mind. I wasn't sure what to say. I didn't really understand what I was feeling.

"I've seen him, Caleb. You might as well tell me who he is," Lilly said.

I shrugged. I could tell she wasn't going to let it go.

"He's my father."

"The man in the wheelchair?" Lilly asked.

"Yep."

"Caleb, I don't understand."

"Neither do I."

"What happened? Is he okay?"

I took a deep breath. I'd never talked about what happened to my dad. Not with my mom. Not with Dr.

175

Ross. Not with anyone.

"He was in a car accident when we lived in L.A. He can't move or talk. He's pretty much dead, but he's not dead."

"Do you mean paralyzed?"

"No. It's different. He's in a vegetative state. The doctor calls it Unresponsive Wakefulness Syndrome. He doesn't talk or move. Just stares and blinks." The fear built up inside of me. It swirled until it clouded my Glow, finally dripping out like sweat drops.

"So, why are you afraid of him?"

"I don't get it, either. I can't be around him. I see him in my dreams. He terrifies me."

"That's sad," Grace chimed in, "My daddy helps me to not be afraid, but you're afraid *of* your daddy. Is there someone else you can think of that will help you not be scared?"

"I don't know." I stared at the ground as a splash of red light swam under my feet. I'd spent so long refusing to think about all of this, I wasn't even sure why I was so afraid. Was I scared that he was gone, or scared I'd caused all of his pain? Or was I scared that he was still very much there and hated me because of what I'd caused to happen to him?

A tear formed in my eye. I wadded up my fist to wipe it away, expecting a black smudge on my arm. The tear wasn't black. Just cold and crystal clear. Not fear. Not guilt. Real, true sadness. A sense of loss. Either he was absent from those empty eyes or trapped behind them because of me.

Either way, I'd lost my father.

G race, would you go and check on Anna and Will? I want to know how much time they think we have left," Lilly said.

"Okay. I get it. Will and Anna had their alone time. Now you want to be alone with Caleb, right? Are you two in loooooove?"

"No, Grace," Lilly said. An expected answer, but still disappointing.

"I wonder if I'll ever fall in love." Grace wandered off.

"She's adorable."

"Yeah." I still couldn't look at Lilly.

"I'm sorry about your dad, Caleb. Was his accident the reason you moved to Ambler?"

I nodded. Another tear dropped from my eyes.

"This all must be so hard for you. All these changes." Her eyes followed a blur of red as it moved between us.

I couldn't talk. My throat was tight, like my neck muscles had wrapped around my windpipe. I'd told Lilly more than I'd told anyone else. I was even crying in front of her. And I wasn't even embarrassed.

We sat in silence, watching the swarms of color glide through the vast blackness.

"Thanks." I finally managed to squeeze out. She smiled at me. But her smile faded fast.

"Do you think we'll be trapped in here for as long as Will, Anna, and Grace? Do you think we'll ever get out?"

"We have to, Lilly. Who knows how long our bodies can live without our spirits in them? We have to take this chance now."

"I need to think positive, don't I? I can't let myself get scared. It's so hard to control, though."

"I guess we need to be like Grace, like you said. We need to think of someone or something that makes us feel safe."

"Who are you going to think of?" Lilly asked.

"I honestly don't know." I shrugged. "How about you? Blake?"

Her jaw dropped open. "Oh yeah, right."

"It's obvious you like him," I said. "What's not obvious is *why* you like him."

She tilted her head toward me, one eyebrow raised. "Why wouldn't I like him?"

"Because he's an idiot."

She threw her head back and laughed. "Oh, Caleb, would you happen to be jealous?"

Was I that obvious? Probably so. My Glow was lit up almost as brightly as the swirling red lights around us.

"No. I just can't stand Blake. That's all."

"Are you any different than Blake? What do you know about me, Caleb?"

What was she talking about?

"I know a lot of stuff about you."

"Okay. What college do I want to go to?"

"Uh. . . ."

"My favorite song? My favorite color? My hobbies? Anything?" Lilly folded her arms, waiting.

"I. . . uh. . . ." There was nothing to do but stutter. I didn't have any answers.

"Did you know I liked Blake when I was younger, but he completely ignored me?"

"What? He's totally possessive of you now. Like a creep."

She nodded. "That's now. Then, when I liked him, I was this hideous awkward thing. My hair was always flaring out, bright red, and my teeth were all crooked. I was thin as a rail and covered in freckles. So, Blake wanted nothing to do with me."

"That can't be true."

"And now, Ta-da! I grew out of it. I look different. So, Blake is interested. It's like magic." She closed her eyes. "Doesn't he know I'm still the same person I was when he wouldn't go anywhere near me?"

"What a jerk," I muttered.

"Are you any different?"

I drooped my head. I wanted to tell her I *was* different than Blake. So much different.

But I couldn't.

"You know, Grace figured it out. I'm not really scared of drowning. I'm scared that no one will come for me when I'm drowning. I'm afraid that, the moment I need someone, everyone will disappear."

"That won't happen. You have lots of friends." This conversation was getting all sorts of personal, like it was spinning out of control.

"Lots of friends? Not when you're ugly. Only when you're pretty. That's how it went with my dad. My mom put on a little weight and stopped wearing make-up and my dad left her for a younger woman. Who's to say that won't happen to me when I get older?"

"I don't know, Lilly . . . I . . . ."

"I mean, who stays pretty? We all get old. We all die. Will anyone care about me if I'm not pretty? Is pretty all there is? What about me, the person inside? Don't *I* matter?"

Dark water oozed from her arms and out of her mouth. She heaved it out, shifting to her knees. I knelt beside her as it formed a stream and slithered away.

What could I say? The old me would've done anything to avoid a moment like this. Too much mushy-gushy emotion.

But I felt it. I felt her sorrow, her doubt. The darkness that filled my heart after my dad's crash became her sorrow from when her dad left. It was cold and heavy, pressing down on me. Pulling me under.

Like drowning.

"I'm sorry, Lilly," I finally managed to say.

"What for?" She wiped her mouth.

"Lots of things. I'm sorry I scared you. I'm sorry I was a jerk. I'm sorry that, because of me, you're stuck here."

"We're not stuck here, Caleb. You said it yourself. We're going to get out."

"I'll do whatever I can to make that happen." It was a promise. The best I could give. And the light that shone from both of our Glows let me know that it was enough. Enough to give us hope.

Lilly moved closer to me.

"I know you will." She stared at me, looking into

me. Again, I couldn't think of one word to say. I stared back at her, a moronic expression on my face.

"Hey you two," said Anna. We hadn't noticed their approach. "We've decided we're going to lure Darkwater here fast."

"We need to get this show on the road," Will said. "And, well shucks, I've always wanted to do this, but I've never been brave enough to try it until now."

"Me too. So. Here goes." Anna pulled Will to her. Their bodies came together.

Will leaned his head away from Anna. "Get ready to run," he said. He pulled Anna closer and kissed her. On the lips.

"Gross!" yelled Grace.

The dullness of their spirits brightened as they kissed. They rose a foot off the ground, spinning in mid-air. The red lights sparkled in a final brilliant blaze, dashing wildly against silver and bronze. Grace, Lilly, and I stood mesmerized.

The red light faded. Will and Anna drifted back to the ground, still holding each other. They both looked a little bit dazed. Will shook it off first.

The air felt cold. The light hadn't just gone, it had been suffocated. Level three became thick with a foamy grey fog.

"He's here," Will said.

CHAPTER

18

Dark rain pelted the metal floor beneath each footfall as we ran for the gap. The drops hissed into steam as they crashed to the ground. The tiny puffs surrounded me, each forming into my father's drooping face.

"Don't stop, Caleb. Don't look at them," Will yelled. I swatted at the haze, smearing away the features. I ran at full speed, bursting through the thin veils of mist.

"How do we get back up?" Lilly shouted. I looked ahead. There was no stack of gears to climb, just the balance wheel ticking, over and over, too high above to be of any help. The rubies flashed a millisecond of red before being completely obscured by the settling mists.

"We run up the walls," Will said.

"We what?" I yelled.

"Remember Caleb, you're dead. You can do it. The

dark water is what keeps us weighed down. You can't be afraid. You have to think of something that makes you happy."

"How do you know that will work?"

Anna smiled. "The first time we walked on the walls was the first time Will told me he loved me."

"That's adorable, but how am I going to do it?" I shouted.

"We're coming to the wall. Better start thinking positive." Will and Anna grabbed hands. It was like gravity switched angles just for them. Their feet pressed against the wall and up they went. Their bodies became brighter with each step. Grace followed them, grinning ear to ear. I guessed she was thinking of her dad.

"We can do this, Caleb," Lilly said.

"I don't know. I can't think of anything." Cold fear spread over me. I put my foot on the wall and kicked it back to the ground. The darkness gathered around me, grasping my shoulders and pulling me into it.

"Caleb, find a good thought. Hurry!" She was already heading upwards, her hair hanging down toward me.

In my mind, I saw her nails rip open a red gash in my cheek. I saw Blake punch me in the face. I saw my two best friends back in California laughing without one thought about me. The darkness behind me formed into a black claw and reached for the orange Glow still burning in my chest.

My father was in his car, on his way to buy my stupid ice cream. The claw opened wide.

"Caleb!" Lilly shouted. I opened my eyes and dashed after the sound of her voice. I looked at her; halfway up the wall. Panic covered her face. She was coming back down. She was coming to save me. Why would she risk her Glow for me?

The answer was simple.

She cared about me.

My mind broke the dark shackle. I ran as fast as I could from the mist.

Lilly reached her hand out to me. I grabbed onto her, feeling strength flow through me as her fingers intertwined with mine. Before I even knew I could do it, I was running up the wall.

Will and Anna disappeared through a rectangular gap between the levels. Grace was right behind them. The mist was gone.

We darted through the gap and found ourselves behind a gear on the bottom of the stack. Anna, Will, and Grace stood waiting for us.

"Darkwater went away." I hunched over, already worn out.

"He's getting ready to pursue us, but he'll never suspect some of us are running toward his fortress instead of away from it," Will said. "Wait until you see him come after Anna and me, then run as fast as you can."

"Anna and you? You said Anna was going to stay with Grace," I said.

Anna shook her head.

"That's not how it's going to work. That's what our little chat was about. If something happens to him, I want to be there with him."

Will gripped her hand tightly in his. "Being together is the only way we won't be afraid for each other. And it's time to stop being afraid."

"Then Grace comes with us." Lilly wrapped an arm around her. Grace smiled up at her. I didn't think that was the best idea, but there wasn't time to argue.

Will tousled Grace's hair with his fingers. "Take good care of them, Grace. Help them be brave."

"I will." Grace's smile was contagious. We were seconds away from entering a fortress made of pure fear and there we were, standing around, smiling like idiots.

"Let's go." Will and Anna dashed out into the small area of open space between the fortress and the gear stack. In seconds, a clump of darkness came after them. They ran, still holding hands.

"Are they going to be okay?" Grace asked.

"Of course they are." I wished I believed my own

words.

Lilly, Grace, and I crept from our hiding place and headed toward the black walls.

The tower loomed before us, shrouded in mist. The gears behind and above us twirled in a synchronized dance. Fear crept into my heart. Fear of dying. Fear of losing my new friends. Fear of trains crashing together in a mass of screaming, twisted metal. Fear of Darkwater.

And, at the top of all of it, fear of my father.

We ran in silence. I tried to think of all sorts of things to get my mind off my fears. Puppies, kittens, hamburgers. Nothing worked.

I thought about Darkwater. He killed Matthew Bradford. He was trying to kill me and Lilly so he could feed off our terror forever. My cold fear melted under a new burning feeling in my chest.

Anger.

We dropped to our knees next to the moat.

"I'm scared." Grace wrapped her tiny arms around herself and shivered. Black mists seeped from her body.

"Remember Grace, think of your daddy," Lilly coaxed.

"Do you really think Will and Anna will be okay?"

"Of course they will, Gracie. Of course they will."

I searched the horizon for Will and Anna. They were visible, although a long way away. They circled the moat. The waters rippled and joined the wave that pursued them. I stared up at the top of the tower. The carved face would've looked kinda regal if it wasn't barfing up black stuff.

Most of the moat water was following Will and Anna, but the never-ending flow from above kept it full.

So much fear.

"I can't stop shivering," Grace said.

"Think of your dad, Grace. Don't be frightened." Lilly's voice quaked as she ended her sentence. I turned to face her and saw why. Dark water oozed from Grace and flowed toward the rippling moat, moving to join the dark waves.

"Oh no," Grace gasped. The waters met. The rippling stopped. For a moment the moat was still.

"What's happening?" I whispered.

"He knows we're here. He knows we're here." Tears welled up in Grace's eyes.

I turned back to the fortress. The waters crashed together, forming a massive wave. It emptied out of the moat and flowed toward us like a tremendous, oily slug.

He was coming for us.

We ran away. Away from our only chance at escaping. Fear crept back into me, swelling in my throat. The cold spread, stamping out my fiery rage with its hopeless foot. My anger hadn't been enough to stand against it.

I couldn't let my fear control me. I had to clear my head.

The dripping mass reared up and then stopped. The roar of a thousand screams bellowed from its surging body. The sound alone, that horrible sound, stopped all three of us in our tracks. I shook uncontrollably. Darkness dripped down my body. I couldn't move. I froze, just staring at the blob of liquid terror hovering over us, ready to crush out any hope I had left.

We had already failed.

The dark water turned from us, sputtering viciously. Will and Anna. I turned to see them. They were floating in the air again. Lip-locked.

The blob of dark water flowed after them like a charging bull. They took off running, still clinging to each other.

They were risking it all for us. We couldn't just stand there.

"Come on!"

Lilly, Grace, and I sprinted toward the fortress. We checked all around us for signs of Darkwater, but he was gone. Will and Anna had done their job well.

We leaped over the empty moat and ran up to the front of the fortress. It writhed and bubbled with darkness.

"How do we get in?" Lilly asked.

"I don't know." How did she expect me to know? Did the fear fortresses of Dreadmongers have front doors? I really had no clue.

"Maybe if we make the fear go away, it will make the dark go away, just like my daddy told me." As Grace spoke, a bit of the wall nearest her became transparent.

"It's working," Lilly said. "Think about positive things, like when we ran up the wall. Come on!"

We moved closer to the wall. Lilly and Grace focused hard. Smiles formed on their faces. I didn't know what to think about, so I just watched them. Just like Grace had said, the blackness in front of them faded away, revealing a shadowy passageway.

"Let's go," Lilly said. We stepped in, cautiously. The wall dripped closed behind us.

We were sealed in.

"That's not good." Lilly stepped back toward the wall. "Do you think it was a trap?"

"I'm not sure."

"Maybe this wasn't the best idea." Lilly slapped her palm against the goopy barrier.

The walls were made of concentrated fear, churning and blistering with screaming faces, apparitions of ghosts, skeletons, creatures, and demons. Interwoven between all of them, a train sped through on a twisted track, belching steam from its stack as it headed toward collision. My father's face appeared amid the images. I looked away. Lilly and Grace stared into the living collage, transfixed. I was losing them.

"We need to focus on those happy thoughts again," I shouted. Lilly and Grace turned back to me.

"How do we get out?" Grace asked.

"We can't leave yet, Grace. We need to be brave. We're only going to get one chance at this." I put my hand on her shivering shoulder.

Lilly nodded. "How do we get to the top?"

"I don't know. Maybe there are stairs around here somewhere."

"What's that up ahead?" Lilly asked. A chamber was carved in the screaming walls. Bars of jagged black rock dropped from the ceiling, arched like spider's legs. A man was huddled against the wall trapped in the cell. Darkness dripped from his body and seeped into the floor of his prison. The walls flashed with images of children laughing and jumping, all dressed in old-fashioned suits and dresses. I recognized some of them. Will was there, holding Grace's hand. Anna stepped on the train at the last second, just before the train left the station.

The scene in the wall changed to chaos, explosions. The screech of metal against metal. The screams of children.

The man's shoulders rose and fell as he sobbed. As

he turned to look at us, I knew who he was immediately. He looked so much like Austin. Same nose. Same crease in his brow when he was being serious.

It was Austin's great-great-grandfather, the engineer of the Shackamaxon.

It was Henry Harris.

CHAPTER 19

W ho are you?" he muttered.

"My name is Caleb."

"You weren't on the train. How did you get here?"

"We were trapped." I stared at him. Why was he here and not with the children?

He rubbed his eyes. "This isn't a trap. This is our eternal punishment."

"No, Mr. Harris. This isn't hell. This is a place that was set up by a mad man."

He shook his head violently, eyes wide. "No. This is hell and I deserve to be here. I'm the one who caused the train wreck. My negligence killed those children." His eyes filled with black tears.

Pieces came together. His journal. Someone gave him the watch.

"Wait. Who gave you the watch you were using

when the trains crashed?" I asked him. He squinted in confusion.

"My boss, Mr. Blackwell. It was a gift."

"No, it wasn't." I nodded at Lilly. She remembered too. It all made sense. The only way the children from the train wreck could be stuck in here. The only reason the accident even happened.

Time.

"It was the watch. It was wrong. Blackwell gave it to you because he knew it was wrong. He knew you would all die, and he's the one who trapped you here."

"Mr. Blackwell? No. He was an odd man, but he'd never do something like that."

"Lilly!" I almost shouted. "Dark water. Black well. Do you get it?"

She nodded. "Like dark water comes from a black well? This guy thinks he's clever. And he's got issues."

"I . . . left late. I was negligent." Harris stared at his wall. The dying faces.

"No. The watch said you were right on time. It was wrong, Henry. Not you." He wouldn't turn around, entranced by the images of death before him.

Grace waved at him. "Hi, Mr. Engineer-Man."

Slowly, he turned at the sound of her voice.

"I believe Caleb. It wasn't your fault." Grace bounced up and down on her toes, her wide smile

195

reflected in his black-stained eyes. He glanced back at me.

"Mr. Harris, we need your help," I said. "We believe there's a way out of this place. We think it's in the tower. Have you seen it?"

He shook his head. "No. I'm the only one here. Here, and sometimes out there. But in the train. Always in the train." He stumbled back to the ground, the blackness dripping down his arms. The floor lapped it up greedily.

"It's not your fault," Lilly said again. It was going to be hard for him to believe us after having it engrained in his mind for so many years.

This wasn't helping.

"Come on," I said. Lilly and Grace followed me away from Henry Harris as he dropped to his hands and knees again, sobbing at the sights that unfolded below him on the floor. Screams as the trains collided.

"We've got to help him," Lilly said.

"There's no time." I led the group to a staircase that spiraled to higher floors. We ran up as fast as we could.

The second floor was different than the first. The area was filled with lavish furniture and the appearance of expensive objects. Paintings adorned the walls, portraits of a beautiful woman devoid of color. A figure sat in the corner. She turned as we came up the stairs.

"Afton!" Grace cried. She ran to the woman and flung her arms around her. The floors trembled as they embraced. Afton pulled Grace away cautiously.

"I'm so happy to see you, Gracie, but we must be very careful. How did you get in here?" As she stood, her long hair fell over her shoulders, surrounding her beautiful face. She was tall and slender, wearing a floral print dress. Although she was transparent, like the rest of us, her eyes still twinkled with life.

"We came in through the wall. I told everyone to think of someone who made them feel happy, and then the wall opened up and we came inside."

"It's not safe for you in here." Afton looked toward Lilly and me, fear in her eyes. It began to drip from them in thick black drops.

"Do you know the way out?" I asked. Afton stared at me like I was crazy.

"There is no way out, child. I wish that there was, but there isn't."

"There has to be!"

"You shouldn't be here. He'll be returning soon. He will be angry with you." Blackness streamed down her cheeks. She was broken, too, just like Henry Harris. She couldn't help us.

"Come on, let's keep going up." I hurried to the staircase.

"No. I want to stay here with Afton," Grace protested.

"We don't have time for this, Grace. We need to move."

Grace slowly let go of Afton's waist.

"Leave, quickly. Before he returns." Afton dropped slowly onto her sofa.

"Let's go, Grace. Now!" I had already started climbing the next set of stairs. She followed Lilly and we ran up another flight.

"No more stopping. These prisoners don't know anything," I shouted.

There were prisoners on every floor. Grace knew most of them. They were with her on the train. She had watched as each one was taken by Darkwater. Reverend Sheridan, Frederick, and a bunch of others, each being terrorized in their individualized torture chambers.

The floors became narrower as we wound our way up the central tower. The sculpted face must've been right outside. The roar of dark water pouring from the mouth came from above us. We were close to the top.

"We're going to make it," Lilly said. Hope sprung up in my chest.

As we rounded the corner of the last floor, the stairway rose above us, looping around the walls of the cylindrical tower. At the very top, there was a crack of light. A break in the glass of the watch face, just above the hands.

Our exit.

We sprinted up the stairs, winding our way higher and higher. I forced myself not to look down. One slip on a stair and the gaping hole in the center of the tower would swallow me.

The walls of the tower began to pulse and ripple. Black bubbles formed and burst around us. One by one, the blobs of darkness took form.

Water. Wasps. My father.

A wave of black water crashed down over my father's wheelchair. The wasps flew through the wave as if it were air, attacking Grace. She screamed. I wanted to help her, but I was frozen. My father sat in front of me.

I couldn't move.

The wasps swarmed Grace as the dark water wrapped tightly around Lilly. Grace swatted wildly as the blobs stung her over and over again.

I tried to pull away from the gaze of my father. His lifeless eyes bored into me.

Grace lost her balance. Her piercing scream rang out through the tower as she slipped off of the staircase and plummeted into the darkness below.

"No!" I shouted.

"Grace!" Lilly screamed. She pulled herself out of

the rippling surge of water. Dark water streamed from her eyes and mouth. I heard it mocking her.

Don't be afraid. Don't be afraid. Ha ha ha!

It pulled her back in and wrapped her up tight. She flailed as it slithered through her mouth and out of her nostrils.

"Lilly!" I shouted. My father stared blankly at me. I had to fight.

Lilly emerged from the water again, coughing and sputtering. The dark water receded from her, recoiling into the wall.

The look on her face. Complete terror. She lay on the stair step, soaked in fear.

"I'm sorry, Caleb," Lily said.

The dark water surged from the wall again. The crashing wave slapped her against the stair step and hurled her over the edge. Her scream echoed as she dropped into the pit below us.

I was the only one left.

My father's dead eyes fastened on me. I felt my body go rigid.

I let my anger toward Darkwater grow inside of me. My lips curled around my clenched teeth.

"I'm not afraid," I said. "I'm not afraid."

He rolled closer, the wheelchair moving on its own. The wheels squealed as he approached, his face sagging.

His blank eyes staring.

My anger fizzled and my fear grew. It was almost like the fear fed off the anger. My body trembled. I tried to look past him, but I couldn't.

Afton was right. There was no way out. Only my father. Only fear.

Dark water poured down my body. The inky goop dripped down the stairs. My father rolled closer. I backed away, my foot slipping off the edge of the staircase.

Darkness swirled around me. I fell for so long. Dread leaked from me like Icarus's failing feathers. I landed hard, wrapped in darkness, on the first floor. I heard Henry Harris cry out.

"Caleb!" Lilly shouted. She and Grace stood above me.

"We need to get out of here," she said.

"We were so close."

"We need to go. Now!"

I jumped up and ran. The dark wall dissolved from in front of me as we barreled out into the murky world outside of the fortress.

"You cannot escape me," came a hissing voice above us. The whole tower leaned toward us, becoming a massive arm with claw-like fingers. We ran, but it dropped over the top of us.

Grace screamed.

We were trapped.

The face on the tower tilted down to look at us, grasped in his massive claw.

"You were foolish to try to escape. There is no escape. You will always be here. This is your eternity."

Its eyes narrowed on us, black with cold hatred. I could feel it in his stare. It was overwhelming. Loss. Failure. Sorrow. Death.

Complete hopelessness.

"Now for your punishment."

"Hey!"

Will stood on top of a rotating gear on a low level platform. Time seemed to stop as I saw him standing there, tall and brave.

"Let them go!"

"Little fool. You dare command me?" the tower snarled.

"I'm not afraid of you."

"You have always been afraid. You always will be."

"No. Not anymore." Will's words were firm, stated like fact. Darkwater looked him over. The world stood still. The claw that held us scurried away, leaving us on our backs, sobbing.

Anna ran to where we lay and pulled Grace from the ground. "Let's go! He won't be able to keep Darkwater distracted for long."

The dark water coiled together into a huge mass of blackness in front of Will. Gallons and gallons of the stuff, screaming with the voices of children.

"Go!" Will yelled.

Anna's eyes filled with tears. Will wasn't going to run. This was more than a simple distraction.

The dark water took form. A massive cobra, almost as tall as the tower itself. The slick tail wrapped around Will, holding him in place. Still, no fear leaked from him. Hope shone from his body, repelling the darkness. He looked the giant serpent right in the eye. It flicked its black forked tongue, menacingly.

"Will, no!" Anna screamed.

Lilly grabbed Grace's hand and the three of us ran faster than I ever have before.

"You have no control over me," Will yelled at the snake. "I'm not afraid of you!"

"Will!" Anna screamed.

I looked over my shoulder as the massive black cobra spread its hood and bore its venomous fangs.

"I'm not afraid," Will shouted.

The cobra struck. Anna screamed.

The serpent threw back its head, gulping up its prey.

Will was gone.

W
ill!"

The snake turned on Anna, its tongue lashing out. Lilly grabbed Anna's arm and pulled her away from it.

"Let me go! Let me go!" she screamed.

The snake seemed content with Will's sacrifice. It didn't even pursue us. Instead, it coiled around the fortress and dissolved into swampy liquid.

I could barely run. The darkness weighed me down. With each footfall, I heard words in my mind.

My fault. My fault. My fault. My fault.

This was my idea. I had convinced Will to disobey the rules. I had convinced them to come with me. We'd been at the top. We had almost made it. But we didn't. We fell. And now Will was gone.

I looked back at Anna. Part of her was gone, too.

We left a trail of darkness spilling from our bodies, dissolving into grey mist behind us. All the hope I'd felt, the nearness to escape, had disintegrated.

There was no hope.

We sprinted up some platforms and jumped across the void, landing on a spinning gear and dropping to its slick surface. Anna was crying, the black drops smeared all over her face. Grace shuddered. Darkness pooled around her on the ground and slithered away.

"We were so close," Lilly whispered.

"He has Afton as a prisoner," Grace said. "He has lots of people in there. That must be where he keeps everyone he takes. That must be where Will is." Grace pushed herself off the floor, wiping away the blobs of blackness.

"He's gone, Grace. He's gone," Anna stuttered. "We'll never see him again."

"That's not true," Grace began. "We saw. . . ."

Anna stood on trembling knees. "What you saw was an illusion! Will is gone!"

Mr. Redmond stood behind us, followed by the other children, crowding onto the platform.

"Darkwater lets you see what he wants you to see. He wants you to go back to his fortress. It makes his job easy." Mr. Redmond crossed his arms over his chest.

Anna ran to Redmond and threw her arms around

205

him, her body convulsing with sobs.

"Briefly, my dear. I know you are suffering, but we can't afford to break any more rules today. I am deeply grieved we lost Will. I could not stand to lose any others." Redmond's eyes drifted to me. Wordless accusations.

Anna let him go and sank back to the floor. She was covered in darkness. It shrouded her. I didn't know what to say.

"Caleb was right about the fortress, Mr. Redmond," Lilly said. "We saw the way out at the very top. There is hope for us to make it back out alive."

Redmond shook his head. "No, my dear, Caleb was wrong. You wandered into Darkwater's fortress, where he has all power. There is no reality there, only what he wants you to see. I've been inside, too. He let me see what I wanted to see as well. It was all just an illusion. Temptation. He wants your Glows. If you continue to disobey the rules of this place, I'm afraid he will have them soon."

I was too messed up to reply. So much pain, guilt, and sadness.

"This place is safe for now. You should rest. You must be exhausted. When you wake, we will head back to camp. We must keep your Glows safe. We'll talk about plans for your escape later. Please, rest."

Mr. Redmond patted Anna on the shoulder and then walked to the center of the gear, followed by most of the children. Anna and Grace followed Mr. Redmond without a glance back.

I lay down, completely wiped out. Lilly lay beside me.

"You aren't giving up, are you Caleb?" Lilly asked.

I choked back tears.

"Was everything we saw a lie? If so, Will sacrificed himself for nothing. We're no closer to getting out of here, Lilly. Our time is running out."

She rolled over to face me. "Are you sure Mr. Redmond is right? I know what I saw, and what I saw was a way out."

"Even if it is a way out, we couldn't get past it. We all fell, Lilly. We fell because we were afraid. Even if it were real, what makes you think we could ever make it out?"

"I've been thinking about that." She bit her lower lip. "I thought I could beat Darkwater since I learned more about why I was afraid of drowning. I couldn't. You know why? Because I'm still afraid, Caleb. Even if we get out, what's the purpose if all I'm destined for is emptiness."

"I don't understand how you can feel like that, Lilly. I know that you've had a hard time since your dad left, but you're a great person. Seriously, you shouldn't feel like that."

"I know I shouldn't, but I do. That's what I mean, Caleb. The fears that Blackwell preys on aren't simple fears. They run deep. If we're going to beat him, we need to do more than just understand our fears. We need to confront the true fear. Like Grace said, I'm not really afraid of drowning. I'm afraid of abandonment. I'm afraid of being abandoned over and over again until I die."

Lilly concluded with a stark resolution I'd never seen in her usually gentle eyes.

I saw hope.

"I'm working on it. I know I can see my life differently. You need to work on it, too. What's behind your fear, Caleb?"

I didn't answer her. I didn't know the answer.

"I've told you all of my secrets. Tell me yours."

Dr. Ross thought I felt responsible for my father's accident. Of course I did. He left the house that night because of me. He left because I wanted a stupid ice cream flavor. It was me. I killed him. I killed Lilly. And I'd just killed Will.

My brain hurt. My eyelids started to close.

"I . . . don't know, Lilly. I need to rest. Can we talk about this later?"

"Yes. Of course," Lilly whispered.

"I wonder if we'll see Austin." My words slurred.

"I hope so," Lilly answered, as I slipped into sleep. "I hope so."

I was on the dusty floor again. I tried to open my eyes and move my arms. My body refused to respond to me, no matter how hard I tried. I could see straight ahead of me. The room was dark. How long had we been in the watch? Where was Austin?

His face appeared in front of mine immediately.

"Caleb? You're back? Thank goodness. Your mom called. We've been here for around three hours. I keep telling my parents that we keep finding cool stuff to look at. I can't imagine what will happen if they find you here, like this."

More guilt settled in. My mom. If she found me like this, like my dad, it would be too much for her to take.

"Austin, did you learn anything? Do you know how to get us out of here?"

"No. I did some research on those people that you named, though. Found out some interesting stuff. That Afton Wallace you mentioned? She was murdered, Caleb. She was found in her apartment strangled to death about a week before the Great Train Wreck."

"She was murdered? I'll bet Blackwell did it," I said.

"He was a suspect. She was his secretary. The police

found some kind of evidence that pinned the murder on her fiancé, though. Afton's fiancé was found guilty of the murder and sentenced to death. But Blackwell was a suspect. From what I read, a lot of the police still thought that Blackwell did it. Especially since Blackwell killed himself about three days after the Great Train Wreck."

"He killed himself?"

"Yup. Hung himself," Austin said. He stooped down and scratched his head.

"Sorry man. Lilly is here now, too."

"Can she hear you talking to me?"

"Yeah. She can. She's worried you're giving up? You can't give up."

"There's no way out from our end, Austin. You've got to figure this out. When we tried, a friend got hurt."

Austin slapped his forehead. "Caleb, listen to yourself. Your friends are dead. They can't get hurt. Man, the Dreadmonger sure knows how to do his job, doesn't he? You said it yourself, Caleb. It's all drama. He's using your emotions to make it seem hopeless. You have to think like a Dreadmonger, Caleb! I know you can. You scared us to death that night with your little prank. If you wanted people to be scared all of the time, what would you do?"

"I don't know. I'm not that into scaring people, okay?"

"Hold on a second. Hillary is coming. She doesn't believe me right now. She says she's going to call the police if you guys don't wake up soon." Austin's shoulders hunched.

"I thought Hillary believed in your 'gift' or whatever."

"I thought she did too. She's scared. I don't blame her. You guys look kinda dead."

"Austin, you are sick. Now you're pretending to talk to them?" Hillary's eyes were red from crying.

"I am talking to them, Hill. You have to believe me."

"I'm calling the police."

"No, Hillary. If they take their bodies away I'm not sure if Caleb and Lilly will be able to get them back. They need to stay here."

"Fine. I'll give it one more hour, Austin. Then, I'm calling." She stomped out of the room.

"Man, I hope she doesn't call the police." Austin rubbed at his eyes and took in a deep breath.

"Austin, get us out of here and all of your problems will be solved. Find a way!" I shouted.

"I don't know how to do that. I would come in after you, but I can't get the watch to open. I've tried everything."

"Then it *is* hopeless."

"No! It's not hopeless." Austin slammed his fist

down on the dusty floor. "The Dreadmonger wants you to give up. I keep telling you, you have to think like him, Caleb. That's how you beat a Dreadmonger. Figure out what he's doing to make you afraid. Conquer your fears and he will be powerless against you."

Austin turned his head. "Lilly?"

I had to think like Blackwell, like a madman who killed a woman and a train full of kids. Like a man who kept their souls in torment so he could feed off their fear. Like a man who lured Matthew Bradford, Lilly, and me into a watch to torture us, just to add to his own power. How could I think like that? How could I overcome my fear when I didn't even know why I was afraid?

Grace's words drifted through my mind. *Daddy said the more you do something, the less afraid you become.*

If her dad was right, then how come everyone was still so scared, even after all of these years?

And that was it.

I had a realization. I thought like a Dreadmonger. His plan became crystal clear.

"Austin," I called. "I think I may have figured it out."

"You need to wake up, Caleb!"

"But Austin. . . ."

"Something's happened to Lilly. Something bad."

"What happened?"

"I don't know. I can feel it, though. It's like . . . it's

like she just died." Austin's voice was quaking.

"Oh no," I whispered.

"Wake up, Caleb! Wake up and save her!" Austin
yelled. His voice grew distant, and the room faded from
view.

CHAPTER
21

Even before I opened my eyes, I heard the screams. Children darted left and right. Waves of putrid water rose above them and came crashing down in front of me. Within it, I saw an orange glow.

Lilly's Glow.

I jumped to my feet as the wave rushed toward me. The water formed into the melting figure of Darkwater. His skull-like face oozed fear. His stretched neck still crooked from where he had hung himself in life. He had killed himself to get here. Thanks to what Austin told me, I finally had a good idea of why he'd done it. I hoped my theory was right.

"Hello, Caleb," he hissed.

"I'm not afraid of you," I shouted at him. He laughed.

"I know, Caleb. You're not afraid of me. You're

afraid of him."

In seconds, the distorted figure of Darkwater transformed into my father. I stopped dead.

The man stuck in the wheelchair, the man I had loved. He stared at me. There was nothing in his eyes. His chest bubbled and oozed. Fingers formed in the sludge.

Why was I so afraid? I had to figure it out. Now.

An oily black hand emerged from his chest. The fingers wriggled like leeches, reaching for the orange orb in my chest. I had to fight it.

Why was I afraid? Why couldn't I move? I couldn't give up now.

The hand reached into my chest, each finger searingly cold.

I had to stop him. I had to do something.

The fist came out of my chest, fingers wrapped around my Glow.

It was too late. My Glow left my body. I felt myself die.

My father smiled at me, his face bursting open. Black water spouted from his neck and washed my Glow away from me. The wave rippled off, two glowing orange orbs in the midst of it. I fell to my knees.

"It's over," I whispered. "He won."

"No, Caleb. It can't be over. We have to get our

Glows back." Lilly sat up, dark water streaming off her body. Her face was so pale, like the other ghosts in the watch.

Mr. Redmond shook his head. "I'm sorry. I thought we'd be safe here."

Lilly pursed her lips and stared Mr. Redmond in the eyes. "I'm going to get my Glow back."

"No, my dear. Don't make a foolish mistake. You'll be taken."

"I don't believe you." She pushed herself up from the ground and jumped off the side of the gear into the mist surrounding us.

I smiled at Redmond. "I'm going with her. And we won't come back without our Glows."

The children erupted into cheers as I followed her off the ledge. We fell into the darkness below.

We ran as fast as we could, following the trail of blackness left behind by the dark water. I thought about home. I thought about my mom. I thought about Lilly. Her fire, her courage. The Glow that no one could ever take from her. We ran so fast that soon we were gaining on the thick cloud of darkness.

"Let's get our Glows back," Lilly growled.

"I think I know how." We were moving so fast that the wave was just in front of us. It seeped into the fortress.

We gripped hands. Light spread between us, bleeding up our connected arms and into our bodies. Shared hope.

The dark wall split open before we'd even touched it. We sped through the dark wall and into the tower. Henry Harris turned to watch us as we zipped up the staircase.

Why was I so afraid of my father? Was he still there, in that silent body?

I thought of Austin kneeling in front of my body. I was there, in the same room with him, but unable to move or speak. Austin could hear me, but no one could hear my father. My father was trapped. He was trapped in his body like I was trapped in this watch. He hadn't abandoned me.

He loved me.

That's why he went out that night. He wanted me to know he loved me. It wouldn't have mattered if I'd asked him to get me ice cream or asked him to risk his life for me. He would've done it.

Simply because he loved me.

"Are you ready for this Caleb?" Lilly asked me. An image popped into my head. It was my mother. She had stopped me just before I left the house.

I love you, she had said. *Never forget that. He loves you, too.*

"Yeah. Ready."

We sped up the stairs leaving behind a misty trail of dark vapors. The crack was just above us. So close.

Darkwater turned on us. He crashed down on Lilly and me in a rush of liquid blackness, ripping us away from each other. Within the water, bubbles rippled, forming into the vacant eyes of my father. My body froze up. The dark water slid me toward the edge of the stairway.

I looked into my father's eyes. I looked past the dead exterior. He was there. He was trying to say something. He couldn't speak it, but he was trying desperately.

I saw memories in his eyes. My memories. Happy times with him. The time he woke me up super early on my birthday and took me out to breakfast before he went to work. The time we went to the mountains and built snowmen together until our lips turned blue. The time I broke Mom's favorite crystal vase and he bought her a new one before she found out.

My dad's lips quivered. He was still trying to say something. He couldn't get his lips to work. He was trying as hard as he could.

I didn't need to hear it. I already knew what he wanted to say. It was the same thing I would have strug-gled with all of my energy to tell my mother if she were in the room with my motionless body at that moment. It was the same thing she had told me as I left her in tears the last time I saw her.

I love you.

I could move. I gripped the edge of the stairway just as I slipped off. I pulled myself up and back onto the staircase as the dark water cleared away from me.

"Lilly!"

She fell, the dark water swirling around her like a cocoon. Her face was frozen, her mouth gaping.

Darkwater's crooked form emerged from the swell of blackness. He headed for the crack in the watch face, an orange orb in each hand.

Our Glows.

A scowl covered his face as he glared back at me. He leaped through the crack. A seal of dark water spattered across the opening, sealing it shut behind him.

I pushed up against the thick, tar-like spatter. It stuck to my hands but didn't budge. I was so close. I couldn't let him win now.

Think like a Dreadmonger.

If fear gave him power, would it also give me power? Blackwell was running from me now, wasn't he?

I concentrated on the thick band of dark water that blocked my escape. It rippled at me curiously. I thought of Mr. Blackwell, but not as Darkwater. I thought of him as a sickly, shriveled old man. Powerless. Weak. I motioned to the dark water. It slackened but then reformed, thicker than before. I concentrated harder. It trembled and then fell, oozing from the crack, dripping away into the dark pit where Lilly had fallen.

It worked. The dark water was concentrated fear. Now that Blackwell was afraid of me and I was no longer afraid of him, the fear obeyed me.

Light poured through the crack. I emerged into the room from the watch face. My spirit was free, but, without my Glow, I still couldn't enter my body. It lay lifeless on the floor.

Austin stood in front of Lilly, pressing against her shoulders, trying to hold her back.

"Come on, Austin. Let me go. I don't want to have to kill you," Lilly said.

"You're not Lilly." Austin shoved her back. "I won't let you leave."

"Then you'll die." Darkness gathered around her, strengthening her grip as she wrapped her hands around Austin's throat.

"Let him go," I demanded. Blackwell couldn't hear me. He was physical now, bound to Lilly's body. Austin's face went blue, his arms swatting at Lilly as he fought to breathe.

With one thought, the dark water rushed away

from Lilly's hands and limbs. I gathered it by my side, still sloppy at controlling it.

Lilly gawked in my direction. She dropped Austin. He slapped to the ground, gasping for breath.

Lilly knelt low, her eyes scanning left and right. She waved her hands and blasts of dark water soared through the room. I dodged easily. Each new blast shot past me and broke into screams on the wall.

Lilly's eyes landed on me and she lunged. Darkness blazed from inside of her like coal black tendrils of fire. Black ripples came out of her face, forming into a snarling skull, grinding its grey teeth with rage.

Instead of running from it, I stood my ground and reached inside. I gripped the crooked neck. It flowed through my hands like globs of dough. Finally, my fingers closed around something cold, pale, and fragile.

The wrinkled flesh of Mr. Blackwater's real neck. Dark water abandoned him as I held him firm. His grey face was bony, lips shriveled around yellowed teeth.

Just an old man. A little, weak man.

With a powerful yank, I pulled Blackwell's spirit right out of Lilly's body. He lay on the floor, two Glows burning brightly in his chest. Lilly's body went limp and slumped to the ground.

Austin sat up. "Get him, Caleb!"

"Give me the Glows," I demanded.

Mr. Blackwell stood, his body dripping with fear. He growled at me.

"I'm not afraid of you." This time I wasn't lying. He knew it. The dark water huddled in the corners, unresponsive to him.

"Take it," he snarled. He reached into his chest and pulled my Glow from within. He tossed it to me.

"I see it was a mistake to bring you into my realm. I am glad to be rid of you."

"Let Lilly and the others go."

He ground his teeth. "You have your life back, now take it. They are mine." Blackwell leaped toward the watch and disappeared into its face. It clamped shut behind him.

The Glow in my hand felt so good. It pulled me magnetically toward my body. I had won. I was free. I could go home to my mom. The nightmare was finally over.

But it wasn't.

Lilly's body lay still on the ground. Her face was pale. I drifted my spirit hand over her cheek and felt nothing. Could I leave her like this? After all the darkness we'd experienced together?

I hadn't made it out of the watch on my own. It took the sacrifices of so many others. Will's bravery. Anna's devotion. Grace's lessons on overcoming fear.

And then there was Lilly. She was the one who'd finally helped me face my fear. My real fear. She was the one who helped me see that my father loved me.

And now she was alone. Abandoned again. Her worst fear. She would be hopeless; trapped forever. I wouldn't leave her. I wouldn't leave any of them.

They had suffered enough.

"Austin," I called.

"Yeah?"

"I'm going back in."

Austin scanned the room trying to locate my spirit. "You can't. He sealed the watch again."

"He expected me to go right back into my body, but I'm not leaving without Lilly or those kids. I beat him. He's weak right now."

Austin locked onto my location, eyes staring right at me. "He'll be stronger in his own realm. He controls a lot of fear in there. I can tell he's good at this. He may seal you in again."

"I know. But I'm not leaving them in there."

I glanced back at my body. My face was so pale. Time was short. Soon, my body would take its last breath and I'd be dead for good.

Sweat streaked down Austin's forehead.

"Go save them, Caleb. Before it's too late."

CHAPTER 22

Gears clacked and echoed through the mists as I fell into the darkness. I landed softly back inside the twisted tower. The walls bled into faces. Anna crying, Grace screaming, and Lilly sitting silently, the hope burned out of her eyes. New fears for me.

But I knew the game.

I pictured Mr. Blackwell, pathetic, lying on the ground after I'd torn him free from Lilly's body. The images in the wall faded.

I saw through the prank.

That was it. It was all a prank. A twisted, demented prank.

Thinking like a Dreadmonger was easy. It came naturally to me. I'd come up with so many fear-inducing pranks in my life. Like the time I found a spider and put it on my mom's pillow, or the time I put poppers under the toilet seat right before my dad went in. Or a fake ghost in an old chest at a railroad museum.

The Dreadmonger had been using our fears against us, pranking us. It was time to give him a taste of his own medicine, and I was the master prankster. I knew just what to do.

I concentrated. The dark water responded. It writhed around me like an excited dog whose master had just come home. I commanded it with my mind and it obeyed. The stairs on the spiral staircase flipped down, one by one. I slid down the ramp toward the second floor.

"Afton?" I called. She turned around, her eyes wide with fear.

"What have you done? Blackwell is furious. He's going to punish the children."

"We have to stop him. I need your help."

"I can't leave this room. I've been trapped here for ages."

"He's in love with you," I said. She nodded, her eyes full of tears.

"He was in love with me when we were alive. I wouldn't have anything to do with him, so he trapped me in here. I was the first. He came to me when he still had his Glow." She pointed to the Glow in my chest.

"Before he was dead?"

"Yes. He told me he put me in here so we could be together. Mr. Blackwell told me that my fiancé killed me, but he rescued my spirit. I didn't believe him."

"You were right not to believe him. You were murdered, but Mr. Blackwell is the one who killed you."

"It was hard for me to believe he could do something like that, but, as the years have gone on, it's not so hard to believe anymore." She wiped dark teardrops from her cheek.

"When the children showed up. I wasn't afraid of Blackwell, or Darkwater, like he started calling himself, but what he does to the children horrifies me. I can't control it. I'm scared for them."

"That's how he controls you. He uses them to keep you afraid. In the past, you taught the children how to be brave. They all remember you. That's what they need now, Afton. They need to be brave. You can help them remember. You can free them and yourself."

Afton didn't move. She needed more convincing.

"He can't keep you in here anymore." I focused on the bars of her claw-like prison. They collapsed to the floor in piles of steaming ooze.

"I'm setting you free."

"You can't. I'm afraid of what he'll do to the children. Whenever I do something wrong, he punishes them. We need to obey." Afton trembled.

I focused again. The wall tore open. The stacks of gears swirled and clicked off in the distance.

"Look at all of this, Afton."

She peered out into the world outside of the fortress through the hole I'd opened.

"Do you understand all of this is for you? He brought the children here to make himself powerful enough to live here forever with you. He knows if he can keep all of us afraid, then he can keep you here. That's what *he's* most afraid of. Losing you. We can save them. I beat Blackwell. I've set you free. Now, help me finish this. Help me set them all free."

"His powers get stronger when he's near the children. You may have beat him far away from them, but you will never beat him in here."

"We have to try," I began. Afton wasn't listening to me anymore. Her eyes opened wide and her teeth grit together.

"It's started." She pointed out of the wall. Train tracks were beginning to appear around the edges of the watch. The horrible groan of a steam engine filled the air.

"We need to find them. We can help them fight back. We can end this." I reached my hand out to her.

"He'll punish them if I disobey. I can't."

"Blackwell is already putting them on the train.

What's worse than that? What else can he do to them?"
I asked.

Afton studied my face. Her eyes slowly filled with
more color. "You're right." She nodded her head. "You're
right."

"We have to move fast," I said. "I have an idea."

CHAPTER

I jumped out of the hole I'd torn in the wall, glided down to the ground, and took off running into the murkiness. Dark water flowed around the perimeter of the watch, forming into jagged wooden tracks mounted under smooth steel rails.

I moved faster, toward the stack of gears. I jumped to the first gear and looked out over the vast space above. The skies were clearing up. Blackwell was using all of his remaining dark water to fuel the train wreck.

Finally, I caught sight of them. Right where I'd left them. A mass of tiny bodies. One larger body stood before them.

Mr. Redmond.

I jumped up the gears. It became more and more difficult the closer I came to the children. Afton was right. The children's fear was so strong that Blackwell had total control over the dark water when they were near.

Below, the tracks were nearly complete.

I leaped to the right and landed on the platform. Mr. Redmond ran to me, followed by the whole crowd of children.

"I had heard that you'd gone," Mr. Redmond said.

"I did. But I came back."

Lilly rushed to the front of the crowd. She looked at my orange glowing chest and smiled.

"You got it back."

"Yep. Now it's time to get yours."

"You shouldn't have returned, Caleb. He'll come for you." Redmond's face wrinkled around the edges. His lips trembled.

"I'm not afraid of him anymore. And none of you need to be afraid of Darkwater anymore either." I stepped closer to the crowd of children.

Anna pushed Grace behind her. "How can you say that? You saw him take Will!" She pointed at the tracks forming below us. "We're going to die again! It's your fault, Caleb! All of it!"

"No, Anna. Darkwater didn't take Will. Will was trapped in the tower. I let him out. I let everyone out of the watch."

Anna covered her mouth with a trembling hand.

Redmond's eyes went wide. "What?"

"Yeah. There was a lady trapped in the tower, too. And a bunch of other people. I let them all out. They left."

Redmond's body gave off a black essence. He forced a smile. "You can't do that. You'd have to over-power Darkwater."

"I did. That's how I got my Glow back. I got out and came back in. I let them out. Now I'm going to get everyone else out, too."

Redmond stood very still, staring at me. Probably trying to decide if he believed me or not.

I stepped closer to him. "The lady. I sent her out first. She told me her name is Afton."

Redmond scowled, his body trembling.

Grace ran to his side. "Mr. Redmond? Are you okay?"

Redmond pointed a withered finger at me. "You lie!"

I leaned into his face. "Why don't you tell them the truth, Redmond?"

"You foolish boy. You don't know anything. Don't you see what is happening? It's the train! Darkwater is going to make the children ride the train and it's all your fault!"

The children began to tremble. Dark water spilled

from their pores.

"Tell them who you really are."

"What're you talking about, Caleb?" Anna asked.

"We won't stop being afraid of the dark if we spend most of our time in the light, right Grace?" I continued. "The more you do something, the less afraid you become. When Redmond is here, you don't have to deal with your fears."

"You don't know what you are talking about!" Redmond backed away from me.

"You make them feel safe, so they'll stay afraid."

Anna shook her head. "That makes no sense."

"A Dreadmonger feeds off fear. People adapt. If we were in constant fear, we'd adapt. You knew the children would produce more fear if they had periods of safety. You even named yourself Redmond, which sounds a lot like Reverend. You set yourself up as their guardian, but it was all a lie."

Redmond took another step away from me.

"You were the lure and the trap. You've been lying to these kids, but I'm not lying to you. I *did* let all of your prisoners out."

Redmond quaked from head to toe. His light blue suit darkened and cracked. His face smoldered and broke open, bits of it flaking into the sky like ash.

"Afton is gone," I said.

A shriveled old man emerged from underneath the crumbling layers of his dark water disguise. His pale face was covered in hate and wrinkles. His white hair stood tall and spiky off his balding head. His bones showed through the crumpled black suit he wore. Orange light emanated from beneath his oozing chest. I reached toward the light. His hands wrapped around my wrist, but he couldn't stop me. I pulled Lilly's Glow from his withered rib cage. He fell backward.

"Darkwater," gasped Anna.

"Afton is gone." I stared into his blank white eyeballs.

"Noooooo!" He threw himself off the side of the gear and was caught in the air by a wave of dark water.

The children shivered. There was so little time.

"It worked," I shouted. "You can come out now."

From a gear twenty feet above, people descended toward our group. Afton. Reverend Sheridan. Some children. Will.

Anna screamed and ran to Will, throwing her arms around him. The children gathered around Afton, the Reverend, and the others who'd been taken, smiles beaming from ear to ear. The people they loved. The people who they were told were gone forever. They were here.

They were hope.

"I thought. . . I thought that you abandoned me, too," Lilly said. I handed the glowing orange ball of light back to her.

"Never."

Lilly's Glow burned bright as she put it back into her chest.

A train whistle shrieked through the watch, echoing through the belly of churning gears. Every head turned toward the dark tower.

"Don't be afraid." Afton gathered the trembling children in her arms.

"We can't help it," Grace said. "This is how we died. This is how we came here."

"Well, we're leaving. All of us," I said.

"You said they all got out. Why are they here?" Anna asked.

"Yeah. I was lying." I smiled at her. "Blackwell gets weaker when he's afraid. His greatest fear is Afton escaping. He just got pranked."

"But can we really leave? Can we really make it out of here? Or was that another lie?" Anna pulled Will closer.

"Yes. We can leave. But we have to go now. We can't let Blackwell get us back on that train. If he gains that much power, I'm not sure I'll be able to stop him."

"What are we waiting for? Let's go!" Will pulled

Anna to the edge and, still clasping hands, the two of them jumped off. We all followed, ready to run as we hit the ground.

But we never did.

In the blink of an eye, we were on the train. Henry Harris stood before me, black tears pouring down his face.

"Not again. No, not again!" he said.

Blackwell had seen through my prank. His worst fear had only distracted him for a moment. Not long enough.

The train lurched forward. The children trembled. Tears gushed down Grace's face.

"Don't be afraid, everyone! We can beat him!" I yelled.

The ground shook violently. I fell to the floor of the train engine. All around me, the children screamed. I looked above.

Blackwell's fortress shattered.

It exploded into a cloud of debris like it had been hit by a wrecking ball. Chunks of solid fear rained down on us. As it landed, it melted into dark water. Gallons and gallons of it. It filled the floor and overtook the train, wrapping us all in its greedy tendrils. Screams, cries, and wailing surrounded me. Amidst the chaos, Blackwell laughed.

The dark water rippled into images. Skulls, wasps, vicious wolves with bloodied jowls. The children screamed and cowered in fear. Dark water fell around them, swirling into more of their worst fears. Lilly struggled to keep her head above the rising mist that threatened to pull her under. Wasps surrounded Grace, lunging at her arms again and again.

"Don't pay any attention," I shouted. "Blackwell is just trying to scare you. We can't let him win."

It flowed over me, slapping me back to the floor. In the wall of blackness, I saw Lilly's body lying in the museum, dead still. Austin sobbed next to her. I heard more sobs. My mother. She knelt next to me. We were dead. We had failed.

No. I wouldn't let him control me again. I pushed back. Different images swam through my mind. Lilly and I were alive. I talked and laughed with my mom at the breakfast table. Five-year-old me sitting in a movie theater next to my dad. His hand was large and warm. I was safe. I was loved.

The dark water's grasp on me weakened, and I decided to hit Blackwell with a taste of his own medicine.

I visualized all of us leaving the watch. All of us. The children. Matthew Bradford, Henry Harris. Reverend Sheridan. Last of all, Afton looked back over her shoulder as she slipped out of the crack at the top of the stairwell. We were free. Blackwell was sealed in here by himself. Alone with his fears.

That did the trick. Blackwell appeared in front of me. Dark water danced angrily from his face and body.

"You thought you could trick me? I'll kill you!" He reached out for me, thrusting his tar-like hands into my chest.

I grabbed his writhing wrists before his leech-like fingers could wrap around my Glow. "I'm already dead, but nice try."

"I don't need to keep you in here, Caleb Meyers. I just need your Glow." He leaned in, forcing his hands further inside.

"That's not all you need." I tightened my grip on his wrists. "You need Afton."

Blackwell's eyes blazed with rage. He tore at my chest, trying to reach my Glow.

I laughed in his face. "You're the one who's most afraid. You're afraid to lose her. That's why you created this place. You thought you could force her to love you, but you can't. That's why we're leaving. All of us."

Blackwell roared like a dying animal. His eyes opened wide and he thrust his arms into the air.

"You'll never take her from me!" He leaped from the train into an inky blob of blackness.

Lilly pulled herself up as the dark water receded

from the train. Black strips of tears flowed from the children's eyes. The train's whistle blared in our ears.

"He's too powerful, Caleb. Even now." Anna stood up and braced herself against the train's wall.

"Where's Afton?" I shouted.

Grace stumbled forward, pulling on Afton's arm. "Here she is."

The train lurched forward. Children screamed.

"Afton, sing with them," I said.

She turned to me, her face streaked with tears.

"It's too late."

"No. It's not. Sing with them!"

"I can't," she cried. This was it. Our last chance. I had to think of something.

Grace wiped the tears from her eyes. She grabbed onto Afton's hands.

"We can do this, Afton, we just have to be brave." Grace wrapped her tiny arms around Afton's waist.

Afton wiped Grace's tears away. She took a deep breath. "Oh, my brave young girl. You are right."

And she sang.

"*Awake our souls! Away our fears!*"

Her voice was beautiful, like a songbird.

The train sped up, its ravenous engine glowing orange with burning coal.

Anna blotted her black tears and joined in.

"Let every trembling thought be gone!"

The other children listened in awe. They added their voices to the angelic song.

"Awake, and run the heavenly race,
and put a cheerful courage on!"

We rumbled over the tracks. Black mist poured from the smokestack.

"Louder!" I yelled.

The voices of the children swelled above the clanking engine as they gained confidence. Henry Harris's sobbing stopped as he listened quietly.

Afton put her arm around my shoulder. Lilly held Grace tight. The trains were so close. Anna and Will were kissing again. Blackwell's power was thinning. The children sang louder, their voices breaking up what was left of the murky fog.

"No!" Henry Harris cried out. The Aramingo came around the corner, hurtling toward us at a frantic pace. The singing stopped. The children screamed.

Blackwell was at the helm again, back to his same old tricks. Dark water fell from the children as the train hissed closer to us.

Will clamped his hand on my shoulder and smiled. "I'm not afraid."

Anna smiled. "Me neither."

"Me neither!" Grace stood up.

All around us, children stood tall, faces to the sky.

"I'm not afraid!" we shouted together. Hope shone brightly from us. Lilly grabbed my hand and held it tight. Her eyes danced with dazzling light.

Even Henry Harris smiled.

Just as the trains should have collided, I focused on the track. I concentrated and the dark water obeyed. The track snapped in two, the halves bending away from each other. New track sprouted from the broken edges, angling both engines into the sky. The Shakamaxon and Aramingo chugged into the air, sliding past each other instead of colliding.

The children cheered. Blackwell shrieked. I waved my hand and the track beneath the Aramingo disintegrated. The black train dropped from the sky and splattered to the ground below.

I held Blackwell in a glob of fear. He screamed as he struggled against it. Another motion of my hand and the dark water slammed him to the floor of the Shakamaxon at my feet.

"Let me go!" Blackwell screamed.

"It wouldn't be fair to set everyone else free and leave you here."

"No! I'll die!"

"I know." I smiled at him. "Finally."

He struggled against the dark water, but it was no

use. He wasn't going anywhere.

We shot through the sky, passing spinning gears and whirling spindles, straight through level one. Afton and the children started singing again, taking up where they had left off.

"Swift as the eagle cuts the air,
we'll mount aloft to Thine abode,
On wings of love our souls shall fly,
Nor tire along the heavenly road."

We sailed by the massive hour and minute hands. I closed my eyes as we hurtled toward the glass.

"Nooooooo!" screeched Blackwell.

We crashed through the tiny crack. The glass of the watch face shattered. Shards rained down around us as the train burst free from the old brass pocket watch.

CHAPTER

24

The Shakamaxon grew to its normal size, filling the room. We rolled past Austin who stood in amazement. He shut his eyes, sensing all of us in the room, his smile growing wider and wider.

"You did it, Caleb!" he shouted.

We rode through the building and out, making our way toward the restaurant where the original train station once stood. The place the train should've arrived all those years ago, but never did. Henry Harris blew the whistle as the brakes squealed.

We were inside the restaurant. I squinted as we rumbled through walls, tables and chairs. Our ghost train didn't even rustle a tablecloth. Being completely immaterial had its benefits.

The Shakamaxon skidded to its final stop.

The restaurant was empty and dark, closed for

the night. The red brick walls were covered in old-time pictures of the railroad.

The old station materialized inside of the restaurant. A wooden platform by the tracks, a sturdy ticket booth with a window upfront.

The children were silent, mouths wide, their eyes filled with tears.

Tears that were pure white and sparkled with joy.

Lilly gasped. The platform filled with spirits.

The families of the children.

They had been waiting for them. Waiting for so long.

The train let out a gust of steam as the children hurried out from the side of the train into the arms of their families. A massive man reached out to Grace and she jumped into his arms.

"Daddy!"

All around us, the spirits whispered and wept. Blackwell wormed his way out of my grip and made a run for it.

"Hey!" I shouted.

Henry Harris and Reverend Sheridan were there in a flash. Blackwell tried to conjure up some fearful images from the remaining dark water that clung to him, but it burst into grey poofs and dissolved into the sky. Harris and Sheridan held him tight. Blackwell writhed and

243

screamed.

"Oh, come now," said Reverend Sheridan. "You've been so fond of causing fear, Mr. Blackwell. Now, you get to face your own."

"No!" Blackwell cried. Then he fell silent. I followed his gaze. In the corner of the station, Afton stood with the spirit of a man. He was tall and handsome. I could only assume it was her fiancé. Even after being wrongfully executed for her murder, he had waited for her.

"Afton," Blackwell murmured. She didn't even look at him. She stood still, lost in the eyes of the man she loved. She walked toward the wall hand-in-hand with her fiancé. They disappeared.

Black drops fell from the eyes of the twisted little man with the crooked neck. Sheridan and Harris dragged him away toward a brick wall. Then, they walked right through it. A spatter of dark water dripped to the ground as Blackwell disappeared for good.

Lilly stood by my side as we watched the families walk away. They embraced and vanished as they passed through the train station wall. She reached for my hand.

I glanced at her Glow. It was fading. We were in the restaurant, but our bodies were in the museum.

"We'd better get back," I said. She nodded. We stepped down from the train.

Will and Anna's families talked excitedly. Will

grasped Anna's hand. They turned to us and waved.

"I guess you two really were my lucky stars," Will said. "You made my wish come true."

"Couldn't have done it without you." I smiled.

"You take care of each other," Anna said.

"We will." Lilly and I walked toward the doorway as we watched them disappear through the wall.

Matthew Bradford caught up with us, just as we came to the doorway.

"Uhh, guys? If you can, please tell my parents and my little sister I'm sorry."

"Sure Matthew. We'll find a way," Lilly said. He nodded and headed for the wall. Alone, but happy.

"Let's go." I turned back to the doorway.

Grace stood there, blocking our way. She ran to Lilly and wrapped her arms around her waist. Her massive dad and tiny mom stood by the red brick wall, waiting.

"I love you both," Grace said. "Thank you for saving us."

"Goodbye, Grace," I said. "I'll always remember you when I need to be brave."

Grace smiled. Her parents beckoned to her. Her brothers and sisters crowded around. Then, they also vanished, joining the happy group of reunited families.

Lilly and I rushed through the doorway. Our Glows were fading. We had to move.

Just as we were about to leave the station, I noticed a short, older woman leaning against a wooden sign on the wall. She was dressed in a white bonnet and a black, lace trimmed dress. I recognized her. She nodded at me and then disappeared.

"Was that . . .?"

"Mary Ambler," said Lilly. "I guess she's still trying to help the people who were in that train accident."

We ran to the museum. The shattered watch lay on the ground near our outstretched hands. The golden lid was bent open. Vapors of dark water fizzled from the broken face. Austin leaned over us, desperately trying to sense our spirits.

"Lilly? Caleb?" he shouted.

"Ready?" Lilly asked me.

"Yep."

We stepped into our bodies. For a moment, everything went dark.

Then I heard a ticking.

No, a pounding. It was my heartbeat. My lungs took in oxygen and pushed it back out. My brain hurt, and my throat was burning, but I'd never been so glad to feel pain. I sat up and rubbed my head. Austin looked like he might wet himself with relief.

"You made it back. Oh, my gosh! I didn't know how I was going to explain all of this. Now I don't have to!

You're back!" He wrapped his long, gangly arms around me. He smelled bad. I'm sure I was rather fragrant myself. Lilly sat up, rubbing her temples.

"Lilly!" Austin pushed me aside and grabbed Lilly in a bear hug. She laughed.

Hillary ran into the room. She wiped her tear-stained cheeks. "You guys are okay! Austin wasn't lying!" She ran to us and hugged us too.

"We need to get home. How long have we been gone? Our parents—," I began.

"You guys have been in that watch for five hours. It's about midnight now."

Five hours? It felt like a lifetime.

I tried to stand but immediately lost my balance. Austin cracked open two bottles of water and handed them to us.

"I figured you'd need something to drink first," he said. I took the bottle and let the cold water wash down my parched throat. My stomach rumbled and I needed to go to the bathroom.

"Your parents are so mad. They're driving over here to pick you up." Austin smiled. "I kept telling both of your moms that we were busy working on the museum and finding artifacts and that you couldn't answer your phones. They didn't like that. I'm super glad I don't have to explain your dead bodies, but I still don't think they're ever going to let you hang out with me again."

"Yeah." I laughed. "We're going to need to make up a better story than that."

"Yeah, let's do that. But first, you need to tell me the real story. Everything." Austin stared at us.

"Yeah. Everything." Hillary sat down beside him.

It was obvious they wouldn't take no for an answer.

CHAPTER
25

Despite the season, it was a sunny day in Ambler, Pennsylvania. We cruised down the bumpy road, Mom and me.

"Are you sure you're ready to do this?" Mom swerved the car right at an intersection.

I nodded.

We weaved through the Saturday traffic and slowly thumped over a speed bump, entering the parking lot of the assisted living facility.

Where my dad lived.

"Are you sure, Caleb?" Mom asked again. Her eyes were already watery.

"I'm sure, Mom."

The convalescent home was an orange building that looked cheery but smelled like urine. We walked through the corridors and finally arrived at room twenty-two. Mom cracked the door and peeked in.

"Knock knock," she said, pushing it wide open.

My dad sat in his wheelchair. I felt my heart jump into my throat. That same old feeling returned. Goosebumps and a chill running up my spine. He stared straight ahead with vacant eyes.

I couldn't help it. I was terrified.

I couldn't move.

Grace. What had she said?

The more you do something, the less afraid you become.

My muscles twitched. I took a deep breath and stepped forward.

"Look who came to see you," Mom said. I waved at him. He was motionless. I sat on the bedside next to his wheelchair.

"Hi, Dad."

No response. Mom wiped her eyes.

"Can I talk to him alone?" I asked.

"Well, yes. Okay, honey. If that's what you want. I'll just go get some candy bars from the vending machine in the lobby, okay?"

"Thanks, Mom."

Mom closed the door behind her as she left the room. Her heels click-clacked down the hallway echoing through the corridors of the Ambler Convalescent

Home.

"Hi, Dad." I stared into his blue eyes, trying to find him. "I haven't been to visit you in a while. I'm sorry for that."

No reaction.

"I guess I felt like if you wanted to come back to us badly enough, you would. I thought maybe you blamed me for this."

I examined his eyes again for any sign he could hear me. Nothing. I continued anyway.

"I was scared. Scared that everything you are is gone because of me. If I had just told you to stay home that night. If I had just told you to forget the ice cream. If I had. . . ." I trailed off, tears stinging my eyes.

Dad didn't even twitch. Could he hear me?

I went on anyway. "I learned a few things lately. I learned when you care about someone, you do your best to make them happy. Little things, like ice cream on a birthday. Big things, like risking your life. It's no different in your mind. It's all the same."

I scooted closer to him. "I really was afraid, but I'm not anymore. I know it's not fair. And I know it's not my fault."

I wiped my eyes as the tears fell. "I want you to know I'm here for you now, Dad. You'd have done anything for me. I understand that now. Because you love me. I want you to know I love you too."

His eyes didn't move. His mouth hung open.

"No matter what, I love you. Always remember that."

He sat still. I wiped more tears away.

"Can you hear me, Dad? Can you just give me some sign you can hear me?"

Nothing. Not a flinch. Not a twitch.

Nothing.

I buried my face in my hands and let it all loose. The fear. The guilt. The sorrow. Darkness flowed out of me like it had in the watch.

When I looked up, something had happened.

A single tear formed at the corner of Dad's eye, slowly. I watched, my heart thumping in my chest. It spilled down his cheek.

"Thank you, Dad. That was all I needed." I wrapped my arms around his neck and kissed his sagging cheek.

My mom walked in with one of the orderlies. She pulled a tissue from a nearby box and wiped my dad's eye.

"Sometimes they water," the orderly said.

"Must be hereditary," I said as I wiped my own eyes. Mom smiled at me.

We stayed for an hour, chatting with Dad as if he could respond, remembering good times of being together. Soon, it was time to go.

We walked out into the parking lot. The sun was setting behind the old castle on the hill in patches of red, violet, and orange.

"Beautiful, isn't it?" Mom asked.

"Yep."

"Still interested in moving back to L.A.?"

"No way. This is our home now."

We got back into the car and headed through downtown. The neon sign burned brightly against the night sky.

AMBLER.

A train blasted its horn in the distance as it rattled down the tracks, taking its passengers safely back to their families. Each passenger on that train was just like me. They had a heart full of fear and love. We all would have to make a choice about which emotion we would let rule our lives.

I thought of Lilly and the other brave souls I'd met in the old watch. Will, Anna, Matthew, Afton, and, of course, little Grace.

They were finally home.

And so was I.

AUTHOR'S NOTE

The Great Train Wreck of 1856 was a real event. The characters in my story are fictional, even when I've borrowed the names of real people who were in the Train Wreck. I use their names to honor them. This was their tragedy.

Researching the Great Train Wreck and Ambler, PA taught me so much about strength, bravery, and love for those who surround you. Although this was a horrible catastrophe, selfless people like Mary Ambler rose to the occasion and did their best to save as many of the wounded as they could. Situations like these create a strong love and connection to a place. All of my research about Ambler has shown me that its residents love their borough dearly.

May we be brave like Mary Ambler, and rush toward peril to save as many of the suffering as we can.

Acknowledgments

The road to publication has been a bumpy one, but there have been many wonderful people to support me along the way. Special thanks to Christine Morton, the May Family, Jennifer Agard, Josh Swenson, Jason Franz, Chrystal Carver, and Elizabeth Dimit, my wonderful beta readers and critique partners who've helped me shape this story.

To my agent, the unstoppable Colleen Oefelein, who just keeps fighting for me no matter what else is going down, thank you! You're amazing Colleen!

Thanks to Kiri Jorgensen and all of the peeps at Chicken Scratch Books for bringing my story to life and letting me illustrate it as well. Dream come true!

I have to thank my mom. She might be too scared to read this book, but she's the reason I wrote it. Thanks for everything, Mom! I love you!

And, most importantly, I thank my family who've been so patient as I typed and typed and typed and typed. My three boys, Ethan, Aaron, and Alec who grew up watching me chase this dream and especially my amazing wife. I love you, Cara. Thanks for always cheering me on, despite this lifelong dream of mine nearly taking a lifetime. You're the greatest.

ABOUT THE AUTHOR

JARED AGARD

Jared Agard was writing and illustrating books as far back as he can remember. His mother was a school librarian and knew all the best books to read. Now, he teaches Art and Film at the Beaverton Academy of Science and Engineering in Beaverton, Oregon, which is his dream job, besides being an author. He values creativity and always has a new idea rattling around in his brain. He loves watching cartoons, goofing off with his boys, and chili dogs.

He is married to the most gorgeous woman on the planet and has three amazing boys, two tiger oscars, and the most pathetic dog you've ever seen.

CHICKEN SCRATCH READING SCHOOL

Dread Watch – Novel Study Course

www.chickenscratchbooks.com/courses

Join us at Chicken Scratch Reading School for an online Novel Study Course for *Dread Watch*. Created by certified teachers with extensive curriculum design experience, this offering is a full 6-week course of study for 5th-8th grade students. It includes a close reading focus, comprehension quizzes, vocabulary work, thematic and writing device analysis, a written essay, and culmination project of the student's choice. The course includes a mix of online and on-paper work, highlighted by instructional videos from the author, Jared Agard, and publisher Kiri Jorgensen.

Chicken Scratch Books creates online novel study courses for every book we publish.

Our goal is to teach our readers to appreciate strong new traditional literature.